F
MULDROW

Muldrow, Diane.

Stirring it up.

$13.99

000048590
02/14/2011

DATE			

friends, cooking, eating, talking, life.

Chef!

Grosset & Dunlap

For Bonnie Bader, collaborator, editor, friend—D.M.

Thanks to Kristina Williams, age 10, for her help with "instant messaging-speak" and her contributions to Chapter 1; Jennifer Terrell for so enthusiastically sharing her culinary expertise and advice; and Firefighter Tom Molta, Rescue Company 1, Hoboken, New Jersey, for his helpful technical guidance in Chapter 9. Thanks also to Kari Muldrow, a.k.a. Mom, Rob Muldrow, and Sheila Williams for their cooking and safety tips.

Special thanks to Debra Dorfman and Doug Whiteman.

dish #1

Stirring It Up

ends, cooking, eating, talking, life.

By Diane Muldrow
Illustrated by Barbara Pollak

Grosset & Dunlap
New York

GROSSET & DUNLAP
Published by the Penguin Group
Penguin Group (USA) Inc., 375 Hudson Street, New York, New York 10014, U.S.A.
Penguin Group (Canada), 90 Eglinton Avenue East, Suite 700, Toronto, Ontario,
Canada M4P 2Y3 (a division of Pearson Penguin Canada Inc.)
Penguin Books Ltd, 80 Strand, London WC2R ORL, England
Penguin Ireland, 25 St Stephen's Green, Dublin 2, Ireland
(a division of Penguin Books Ltd)
Penguin Group (Australia), 250 Camberwell Road, Camberwell, Victoria 3124,
Australia (a division of Pearson Australia Group Pty Ltd)
Penguin Books India Pvt Ltd, 11 Community Centre, Panchsheel Park,
New Delhi - 110 017, India
Penguin Group (NZ), Cnr Airborne and Rosedale Roads, Albany, Auckland 1310, New
Zealand (a division of Pearson New Zealand Ltd)
Penguin Books (South Africa) (Pty) Ltd, 24 Sturdee Avenue, Rosebank,
Johannesburg 2196, South Africa

Penguin Books Ltd, Registered Offices:
80 Strand, London WC2R ORL, England

2007 Edition
Cover photos © Image Source

The Library of Congress has cataloged the original edition
[ISBN 0-448-42815-6] as follows:
Library of Congress Control Number: 2002102930

ISBN 978-0-448-44526-7   10 9 8 7 6 5 4 3 2

Molly Moore was starving. And bored. With a yawn, she opened the large chrome refrigerator door, hunched over, and peered inside. Only her long, skinny legs and sky-blue board shorts could be seen.

"What's in there?" asked her twin, Amanda, who sat at the kitchen table, flipping endlessly through a teen music magazine.

Amanda was answered by the clinking sounds of Molly rummaging from shelf to shelf, moving a jar of mayonnaise, pushing back the butter dish, sliding forward a sticky jar with three lonely dill pickles floating in their juice.

"...Um, Molly? Are you in there?"

"You don't want to know what's in here," Molly finally reported in a muffled voice. "A piece of cold pizza...some old pancake batter...Chinese takeout from last week—"

"No, that was from *two* weeks ago," interrupted Amanda. She tossed the crumpled magazine aside. "Remember? We had it after our piano lessons?"

Molly finally backed out from the fridge and turned

around, carrying the white carton of mystery food. Holding it straight ahead, as far from her freckled nose as possible, she made a funny face as she opened the carton. The smell escaped into the air. It was of something old. Something forgotten. Something...rotten!

"*Eeewww!* That was from before we even knew *how* to play piano!" exclaimed Amanda as the odor hit her nose. She stood up and walked over to her sister. "That doesn't even look like food anymore. It looks like—"

"A science experiment!" joked Molly. "*Yecch!*" Crinkling her nose, she quickly dumped the oozing, dripping fungus-formerly-known-as-food into the garbage disposal and turned it on.

Just then, the phone rang. Amanda grabbed it before Molly could reach it.

"Hello?" said Amanda. "Hi, Mom!...We're fine...No, Matthew's playing at Ben's...You're working late? Dad, too?...hang on."

Amanda turned to Molly and said, "Mom wants to know what we want for dinner. She won't have time to cook tonight. She's going to pick up something."

Molly made a face that told her sister, *Oh, no, not take-out again!* "I don't know," she replied grumpily, drumming her fingers on the table.

Amanda flashed Molly her I-know-what-you-mean look, sighed, and turned back into the receiver. "Mom," she said, "we don't care. Matthew will want Chinese, so maybe we should just get that. But Molly and I are sick of everything there is!...Yes, even egg rolls. You'll cook tomorrow, right?...We'll see you later...It's okay, really! Bye, Mom."

Amanda sighed again and sat down at the table with Molly, who was staring up at the ceiling fan. Molly's green eyes became almost emerald in the sunlight that shined brightly in the big kitchen. Of all the rooms in their large townhouse, the eleven-year-old twins liked the kitchen best. It was large enough for a crowd of friends to gather in, to make popcorn and work on a school project together. Painted a pale, buttery yellow, the walls had accents of deep blue and green tiles that Mom had picked up in Spain the summer she taught there. Colorful rugs shaped like apples and pears decorated the floor. Cupboards with glass doors showed off the colorful, funky old dishes that Mom and Dad were always picking up at antique stores and tag sales. From large scrolled hooks attached to the ceiling, a pretty iron rack held shiny copper pots and pans. It was a place to feel comfortable, safe, happy.

"Earth to Molly," said Amanda. She hated it when Molly got that faraway look, as if she'd forgotten Amanda was there. "Hello? Want me to paint your nails? I have a new glittery color. Sizzling Red Pepper."

"Amanda," said Molly, ignoring Amanda's question, "If

you could have anything you wanted for dinner tonight, what would it be?"

"*Hmm,*" said Amanda. "Chocolate cake?"

Molly rolled her eyes.

"Okay," said Amanda, laughing. "Let me think—"

"I know what I'd have," said Molly. "Remember that chicken I had at Luigi's restaurant last week? I think it was called chicken piñata or something like that?"

"I don't *think* so," said Amanda. She picked up the phone and pressed the speed dial for Mom's office.

"Hello, Mom? Hi, again," said Amanda. "What's the name of that lemony chicken that you and Molly had at the Italian restaurant? On Daddy's birthday?...Oh, chicken *piccata*. Can you spell it? P-i-c-c-a-t-a. Thanks, Mom. Bye!"

As Amanda hung up the phone, Molly said, "Let's look it up."

"Look what up?"

"Chicken piccata," said Molly. "Maybe we can find a recipe online."

"Mom isn't cooking tonight," said Amanda. "Remember?"

Molly just looked at Amanda and smiled. She knew her twin would be able to read her mind just about... now.

"You mean *we'd* make it?" shrieked Amanda. "For dinner?"

"You read my mind," said Molly.

"It's the 'twin thing' again," exclaimed the girls.

"Anyway, yeah!" said Molly. "Let's make it for dinner and surprise everyone!" She got up from the table and walked into the den, where the computer was.

"Um, you're forgetting something," said Amanda, following Molly.

"What?" asked Molly, as she logged on to the Internet.

"We can't cook."

"Actually, Amanda, we *don't* cook."

"Right!" said Amanda, laughing. "Because we *don't* know how!"

"We-e-ll, we made hamburgers once, when Mom was sick," Molly reminded her, not looking up from the computer screen.

"We burned them," Amanda replied. "Remember? Dad practically had to call the fire department."

"...and homemade chocolate chip cookies, millions of times," continued Molly. "And gingerbread once, with Grandma. And blueberry muffins."

"Burned, burned, and burned," said Amanda, counting on her fingers.

"Puh-*lease!*" cried Molly, annoyed. Amanda could be so—unadventurous!

"Look, Amanda, if we have a recipe, like, right in front of us, how hard can it be?" she asked, as she kept typing. "I mean, we can read, can't we? Plus we're having such a stupid, boring summer. All of our friends are on vacation or at camp or in summer school. It rains every time we try to go to the beach. It's not like we have anything better to do. Wow, look at all these choices for chicken piccata. I'll just click on...this one. Hey, it looks easy enough to make."

Amanda twirled her long brown hair around her finger as she squinted over Molly's shoulder at the screen. "Mom would be amazed if we cooked dinner," she admitted. "Maybe we should be helping her out more now. Look at all the stuff you need to make chicken piccata! Lemons, chicken breasts, garlic, parsley, capers...what are capers? Molly, we don't have this stuff."

Molly was scanning the recipe, too. "I know we have flour, butter, and olive oil, and we probably have enough money to buy the rest of the stuff," she said as she clicked on the print icon. "Okay, I'm printing this out. Let's go to the store!"

That was it, Amanda realized. Molly's mind was made up. And when Molly's mind was made up, there was no changing it. Nope, better to just go along with Molly's latest scheme—and hope she'd get tired of it sooner or later.

Soon the twins were out the door of their tall townhouse and heading down Taft Street to the supermarket (after Amanda had insisted on taking ten minutes to change her outfit). It was a warm July day, and it seemed as if every kid in Park Terrace was outside, whizzing by on a scooter, a bike, or a pair of in-line skates.

"There's Matthew," said Amanda, waving at their younger brother. "Hi, Matthew."

"Hey, where are you going?" asked Matthew, who was seven. He was riding bikes with Ben. Ben had been Matthew's best friend since the two were toddlers. And Ben's mother, a stay-at-home mom, was Matthew's official baby-sitter.

Matthew was wearing his favorite shorts today, the baggy black ones that Mom had to practically steal from him to wash. And he was wearing a white T-shirt with some sort of monster creature on it (or at least the shirt used to be white; now it always looked dirty, even when it was clean). Yeah, Matthew thought he was all that. Actually, he was all freckles and monster creature bandages.

"You're helmet's crooked," Amanda pointed out to him. As Matthew squirmed and Ben giggled, she adjusted it on his head, saying, "We're going to Choice Foods. 'Cause we're making dinner tonight!"

"You're cooking? *Aaaaaaggh!* Poison!" cried Matthew. He grabbed his throat and made his hazel eyes bug out.

"Don't worry, you can eat at my house tonight, Matthew," Ben said. The boys snickered as they doubled over, pretending that their stomachs hurt.

"Very funny," said Molly as the twins walked away. "See you later."

"*Aaaaagh!*" shouted Matthew, as he and Ben pretended to die agonizing deaths on the sidewalk.

"What*ever*," said Amanda, tossing her hair back and straightening her sparkly lime-green tank top. "Hey, how much money do we have, Molly?"

"...twenty, twenty-one, twenty-two," said Molly, who was counting a stack of one-dollar bills. "Twenty-two dollars."

"Hold it! You're dropping some!" cried Amanda. "Give me the money. You're gonna lose it!"

"Okay," Molly said with a sigh as she handed Amanda the wad of money that she'd stuffed into her board shorts. Amanda was more careful, Molly had to admit. Even though they were identical twins with green eyes, pale skin, long brown hair, and plenty of freckles, Molly and Amanda were very different from each other.

Molly, whose real name was Amelia, (but no one *ever* called her that) liked her thick hair up in a high ponytail, and had to be coaxed into wearing anything other than jeans or shorts. Amanda loved anything girly:

glitter in her hair, velvet tops, colorful jewelry, flavored lip gloss. Amanda was always trying to make Molly try these things, but Molly always seemed to be more interested in something else she had on her mind at that moment. And right now it was cooking dinner for their whole family!

It felt funny for the twins to be in the supermarket without their mom or dad.

"Okay, where should we go first?" asked Amanda, crossing her arms and trying to look cool. "Oh, we have to get a cart."

"We don't need a *cart*," said Molly as she reached for a red plastic hand basket. "We're just getting a few things. Here, take it."

"You can carry it," teased Amanda.

"Okay, Princess," said Molly. "Now," she said, checking the recipe she'd printed out. "Where would the capers be?"

Amanda giggled. "We don't even know what capers are," she said.

"Ask someone," said Molly.

Amanda cringed. "No, you ask!" she said. "Please?"

"Do I have to do *everything?*" asked Molly. "Oh, all right!" She walked over to a woman who had her toddler with her, riding in the shopping cart.

"Excuse me," said Molly in her "important" voice. "Do you know where the capers are?"

"Capers?" asked the woman. "What are they?"

Molly felt her face turning red. "Um, you know—*capers.*"

Just then, the baby began to wail, and the woman turned around and cooed, "Don't cry, pumpkin! Mommy's here! Do you want another cracker? *Hmmm?*"

Molly walked back to Amanda and said, "Just call me The Invisible Girl! Next time, *you* ask."

Just then, a stock boy passed them.

Amanda cleared her throat. "Um, excuse me?" she said. "Where are the capers?"

The stock boy never even looked at the girls. "Capers. Aisle seven," he replied automatically as he quickly started to fill a shelf with canned tuna.

"Watch out! He's a droid," whispered Molly wickedly.

In aisle seven, the girls passed olive oil, dried beans, pasta...

"Look! Capers," said Molly, holding up a small jar of what looked like pickled peas, or little olives. "*Now* I remember seeing these on my chicken—they taste sort of salty and pickle-y. Okay! Let's find the parsley, garlic, chicken stock—whatever that is—lemons, and the chicken. The recipe says the chicken has to be sliced thin, but not too thin."

"How will we know what's right?" Amanda wanted to know. Molly just shrugged. Maybe this dinner would turn out to be a big, slimy mess after all. *Oh, well,* Molly thought, *it'll still be better than being bored.*

When the girls came to the poultry department, they found packages of chicken breasts. Some were very thinly sliced, and some looked fat and juicy. Neither seemed like what the recipe called for.

Just then, the butcher behind the counter noticed the girls' confused expressions. "Hello, there, young ladies!" he called. "Can I help you?"

"Um, yes," Amanda said. "We're looking for thin-sliced chicken breasts. But not too thin. We, uh, don't know which ones to get."

"What are ya makin' with 'em?" asked the butcher. He had rosy cheeks and a full mustache that was almost all white. His blue eyes twinkled. He looked so much like Santa Claus, and he was so *jolly* that Molly had to pretend she was clearing her throat to keep from laughing.

"Oh, we're making chicken piccata," Amanda said casually, as if she cooked gourmet meals every day.

"Wow!" said the butcher. "I'm impressed. Don't look at that packaged stuff. I'll slice up some fresh chicken breasts for you."

"That will be fine," said Molly. That was something their mom would say. The twins looked at each other and giggled.

They watched as the butcher quickly sliced the chicken breasts with a big knife. They looked much better than the packaged ones.

"How many do ya need?" asked the butcher.

The twins looked at each other blankly. They hadn't thought of that yet.

"Well—how many people will you be serving?" asked the butcher.

"Five," said Amanda quickly.

"Okay," said the butcher, packing up the meat in heavy brown paper and weighing it. "Here are seven. That oughtta do it for ya!"

"Thank you!" said the girls.

He handed Molly the heavy square package.

Amanda looked at the price. "It's almost ten dollars!" she said. "That's a lot of money."

"That's what chicken costs, I guess," said Molly. "I hope we have enough money for the other stuff."

The girls didn't need to worry. The chicken stock, which seemed to be kind of like chicken soup, lemons, a head of garlic, and a bunch of parsley weren't expensive.

"Okay, let's get in line and pay for this," said Molly.

"Wait!" said Amanda. "What else are we having besides the chicken?"

"*Oops*," said Molly. "I don't have a clue! Maybe rice, or something like that."

"Oh my gosh!" whispered Amanda. "There's Justin."

"Where?"

"Don't turn around! He's right over there. He's looking at us!"

Justin McElroy nodded to the twins. He was with his mom, who waved to the girls.

"Hi, Justin!" called Molly.

"You don't have to shout!" whispered Amanda, jabbing Molly with her elbow.

Justin was a new neighbor of the Moores. A tall, cute new neighbor who was wearing board shorts with a wild green-and-yellow floral print, and a black T-shirt that said NO FEAR. He was eleven, too, and would be attending Windsor Middle School with the girls in the fall. His reddish-brown hair was short and gelled, his brown eyes were big, and he had that kind of face that always looked like he was smiling, even when he wasn't.

"What are ya doing?" asked Justin, as his mom paid for her groceries.

"Oh, I'm cooking dinner tonight," said Amanda casually. Molly shot her a look that said, *what's this* I'm-*cooking-dinner stuff?* "I mean, Molly and I are cooking dinner tonight," she added.

"Cool. I like to cook, too," said Justin. "Sometimes. Like on the grill and stuff." He picked up two grocery bags and said, "See you later."

"Bye, girls!" said Mrs. McElroy, hoisting a grocery bag. She flashed them a knowing smile that meant, *Isn't my son just the cutest thing you've ever seen in your lives?*

"Wow! A guy who cooks," said Amanda.

"Maybe he'd better come over and teach *us*," joked Molly, as the girls walked back to aisle seven. There they found a package of long grain and wild rice that looked idiot-proof.

"You just throw the rice and the bag of spices in a pot of boiling water," Molly read off the back of the box. "Even Matthew could do that!"

Amanda snorted. "Don't count on it."

Molly laughed. "What else should we make?"

"Salad?" Amanda suggested.

Molly shrugged. "Sounds good. I think we can handle that."

Molly and Amanda walked over to the produce department where they found some fresh lettuce and deep red tomatoes.

"*Mmmm,* an avocado," said Amanda. "This one is ripe—not too hard."

"Great," said Molly. "Throw it in the basket." Soon the twins had paid for everything and were on their way home.

"Here we go!" said Molly as they left the supermarket. "Okay—so you ready to surprise Mom and Dad with the best meal of their lives?"

"It'll be a surprise all right!" said Amanda, laughing. "But what if this turns out to be something that even a dog wouldn't eat?"

Molly's ponytail swung as she laughed and said, "No problem—there's always takeout!"

Molly and Amanda unlocked the door to the house. They carried their groceries into the kitchen, where their fat tiger cat, Kitty, was zonked out as usual on one of the chairs.

A neighbor had given the kitten to Matthew when Matthew turned four. Matthew named her Kitty.

"Don't call her 'Kitty,'" Molly had told him.

"You can name her anything you want!" Amanda had added. "So why would you just call her 'Kitty?'"

"It's his kitten, girls," Mom had told the twins. "That's what most cats end up being called anyway—'Kitty.'"

Thud! Amanda put a heavy bag down on the floor, and Kitty tore out of the kitchen like a shot. She hated loud noises.

"It's okay, Kitty," called Amanda. "Come back, scaredy-cat!"

Kitty peeked around the corner, then creeped back in and sniffed the grocery bag. There was something in there that she liked.

"There's nothing for you in there," Molly told Kitty, shooing her away.

Molly's eyes wandered over to the kitchen clock. "Wow, it's five o'clock already. I guess we'd better get started!" The twins began to take the food out of the bags.

"So—what do we do first?" asked Amanda, looking at the recipe. *This looks so hard,* she thought to herself. *We are NEVER gonna pull this off!*

Molly's eyes moved from the tomatoes to the chicken to the rice. "You know what's gonna be the hard part?" she asked. "Getting all the food to be ready at the same time. How do people do that? Like, how does Mom's big Thanksgiving dinner just—*appear?*"

"Magic," joked Amanda. "No, seriously, it's a mom thing! Moms can just do that."

"Well, we're not magicians," said Molly, putting her hands on her hips and looking up at the pots and pans. "And we're not moms."

"Hey, you got us into this mess, *you* figure it out," chuckled Amanda, turning on the shiny kitchen faucet. "But I think the first thing we should do is wash our hands with antibacterial soap!"

"Oh! We have to wash the chicken, too," said Molly as

she joined Amanda at the sink. "Remember when we saw that on the news?"

"Yeah—otherwise, we might get salmonella poisoning! And the whole family will get sick and throw up! Gross!" exclaimed Amanda. She took out the chicken cutlets and ran cold water over them. "Molly," she said, "Can you put some paper towels down on the counter? That's what Mom does."

Molly tore off big sections of the paper towels and laid them on the counter. Amanda carefully put the cutlets on them to drain. Molly then blotted them dry with more paper towels.

"I guess we'd better wash our hands again," suggested Molly.

"Abso-*lute*-ly," agreed Amanda, reaching for the soap.

"Cool! One thing done," said Molly, walking across the kitchen to turn on the radio. She smiled as she looked at the neat rows of chicken breasts. "Maybe we should make the salad now, and get it out of the way."

So as the girls sang along as loud as they could to their favorite song, they washed the tomatoes with a special liquid to get rid of the chemicals from pesticides. And they rinsed the lettuce and the parsley and dried them off in the salad spinner.

Molly reached for a sharp knife to cut up the

tomatoes with. "Whoa," she said. "I hope I don't chop my finger off."

"Don't let it fall into the salad if you do," teased Amanda. She had a knife, too, for taking the skin off the avocado. The girls worked slowly, because they didn't want to hurt themselves, and because they didn't have a clue about how to properly use a knife.

"How do the chefs on those cooking shows chop everything so fast?" muttered Amanda. The avocado was soft, and seemed to be ending up all over her hands instead of in neat pieces.

Molly picked up the bag of wild rice and read the directions. "This takes only about twenty-five minutes. So we don't have to make this until the chicken is almost ready."

"Then we better start making the chicken now," said Amanda.

"Yeah! Look—it's almost six o'clock! How did that happen?" exclaimed Molly. "Mom and Dad will be home soon."

Amanda slapped her forehead. "Oh, wow!" she cried. "We have to call Mom to tell her not to bring home any takeout!"

Molly frowned. "You're right," she said. "But we wanted to surprise her. How are we gonna tell her not to get any food without spilling the beans? Think fast!"

Amanda picked up the phone. "We-e-ell," she said,

staring out the window, "I guess we'll have to tell her we'll get the takeout for her. But she might not want to let us do that."

Molly's face brightened. "I know!" she shouted. "This'll be a good trick: we'll call Mom. We'll tell her that Dad called us to say that *he's* bringing home the takeout!"

Dee-dee-dee-dee-dee-dee-dee-dee! The phone was making that off-the-hook noise that sounded like a UFO. Amanda quickly hung up the receiver. "But what if Dad calls Mom after we talk to her?" she asked Molly. "She'll probably thank him for getting the food, and he won't know what she's talking about."

Molly shrugged impatiently. "What*ever!* We'll have to take a risk!" she said. "I mean, we've got to call her right now before she leaves her office. Hurry up! We've got a lot to do here!"

"Okay!" said Amanda, nodding her head slowly. "But how do I let you get me *into* these things?" She picked up the phone and hit the speed dial, saying, "I guess you're right. Let's just hope that Mom and Dad don't talk again after we call Mom...Hello? Hi, Mom!...fine...um, Dad just called. Yeah, uh, he really did! He's, uh, bringing home some takeout, so you don't have to, okay? What's he getting? Um, something—fancy! So-okay-we'll-see-you-later—bye!" Amanda quickly hung up the phone. "It's so hard to lie," she said.

"You weren't really lying. Just fibbing a little. She'll understand when she gets her big surprise! Now, let's start the chicken," Molly said.

"Okay," sighed Amanda, turning on the oven. But she still felt guilty.

Making the chicken piccata began easily enough. Molly and Amanda were a good team. Amanda sprinkled each chicken cutlet with salt and pepper, and Molly coated them with flour that she had poured into a dish. Then they heated some olive oil in a skillet, and put several pieces of the chicken in the skillet.

"We have to turn the skillet handle around to the back," said Molly, "so that it's out of the way."

"Now what?" asked Amanda, as the chicken began to crackle and sizzle.

"We have to let the chicken brown," said Molly. "Then we'll turn it over, and brown it on the other side."

"Turn down the heat, Molly," said Amanda. "We don't want to burn the chicken!"

"Or ourselves," added Molly, as she lowered the flame.

After a few minutes, Amanda lifted up one piece of chicken with a pair of tongs and checked it underneath. "Hey, it's brown!" she said. "I'm turning it over."

"Cool!" said Molly. Picking up another pair of tongs, she helped Amanda turn all the pieces over. The chicken sizzled. It smelled good!

"*Mrow?*" cried Kitty, who'd been pacing back and forth. Kitty was absolutely bonkers for chicken. "*Mrow! Mrow!*"

Finally the chicken was nice and brown on both sides. The girls put the chicken on a plate and carefully put it in the oven at a low temperature to keep warm. Then they added the rest of the chicken cutlets to the skillet.

But this time, the chicken didn't smell so good.

"Uh-oh! It's smoking," said Molly. Thinking fast, she put on a thick oven mitt and lifted the pan off the burner. She placed it on a cooler part of the stove.

"I know what we did wrong," said Amanda. "We should've put more olive oil in the pan. There wasn't enough to cook the chicken, so it started to stick to the pan."

Molly took a deep breath. *Don't panic!* she told herself. "Okay," she said. "Let's take the chicken out and heat some more oil." She carefully lifted one piece of chicken out of the pan.

"Please don't be black on the bottom," Amanda pleaded, as if the chicken breast could hear her.

"It isn't!" exclaimed Molly. "Good."

The girls started over. When the oil was hot, Amanda

began to put the chicken back in the pan, using a the tongs.

"*Ooops!*" cried Amanda, as a cutlet slid out of the tongs. It hit the floor with a slapping sound. Molly jumped back, and—

"Whoa!" she shouted, as her elbow knocked the bag of flour onto the floor.

"*Ow!*" cried the twins at the same time. They'd bumped heads as they bent down to pick the chicken off the floor.

"Look at you!" Amanda cried. "You've got flour all over you!"

Molly looked down. The flour was everywhere, all over her rear end and all over the floor. She looked at Amanda, who was still holding the chicken that had fallen onto the floor. Stuck to it was cat hair.

"Oooh, *sick!*" cried Amanda.

That's when Molly cracked up. She couldn't stop laughing.

"What's so funny?" asked Amanda, but then she looked down at the furry chicken and began to laugh, too. Then she rinsed the chicken, dried it off, and salted and peppered and floured it again. "Don't tell anyone I did that," she said, poking Molly with a fork. "Good as new!" she added, as she put it in the skillet with the rest of the chicken.

"That'll be *your* piece," Molly teased her.

Soon all of the chicken was browned. Now it was time to make the lemony sauce that Molly had liked so much. And Mom and Dad would be home soon!

"Yipes!" said Molly. "We'd better start the rice." She took out a pot and measured the water that she needed to boil. Then she poured the rice, and spices that were in a separate packet, into the water along with some olive oil.

Meanwhile, Amanda poured a cup of chicken stock into a measuring cup, then poured it into the pan that they'd browned the chicken in. The next step was to turn the heat back on, add lemon slices, and scrape the skillet with a wooden spoon to loosen the browned bits of chicken that had stuck to the pan. Those little chicken bits would add flavor to the sauce, the recipe explained.

"Now turn the heat back down," said Molly, reading from the recipe. "We have to simmer it now. That means let it cook on a low flame. It's supposed to slowly get thicker. *Mmmm.* This sauce is beginning to smell good!"

Sure enough, after nearly five minutes on a low

flame, the liquid began to thicken and look more like a sauce. As Amanda stirred it, Molly squeezed a lemon and then poured the juice into the sauce.

That's when they heard the front door opening. Mom's and Matthew's voices echoed in the hallway. The twins heard quick footsteps and Mom's jangling bracelets as she rushed down the hallway.

"What's going on?" cried Mom. Her tall frame filled the doorway, and her dark brown eyes were open wide. "What's burning?" Her darting eyes followed the trail of flour.

"Nothing's burning! *Surprise!*" shouted Amanda and Molly.

"Wow! You're—cooking! Uh, wow!"

"It'll be ready really soon," said Amanda. "Oh! We have to set the table!"

"They're trying to poison us, Mom," snickered Matthew. But he came over to the pan and took a deep breath anyway.

"Get out of there, Matthew," Amanda scolded. Matthew must have liked how it smelled, because this time he forgot to act sick.

"It smells great, girls! What is it?" asked Mom. She took her big leather bag off her shoulder and hung it on the back of a kitchen chair, but her eyes never left the skillet that Amanda was using.

"Broiled monkey brains," cracked Matthew.

"Chicken piccata!" cried the twins.

"And wild rice!" added Molly.

"And salad," said Amanda, adding the capers to the sauce.

"Well! I can't believe you did all this! But you could have set the place on fire!" said Mom, unbuttoning the jacket of her brown linen suit. "I'm sorry, but I mean, I hope you were careful. Oh, it smells so good!" She began to laugh. Mom had such a loud laugh that everyone else always started laughing, too.

That's when Dad came home.

"Hel-*lo*, everybody!" he bellowed. Dad was tall and his voice was loud and deep, especially when he came home and greeted everyone. He ran his hand through his graying black hair to mess it up, which he did every night when he got home from work. He didn't seem to know he was doing it, but the twins knew he must have been thinking, *I'm home from work and it doesn't matter what my hair looks like!*

"Mike, the girls cooked dinner!" said Mom.

"It smells great!" said Dad as he kissed Mom and the girls. He hugged Matthew and said, "Hey, champ, how's the new bike working out?" Then he adjusted his wire-rimmed glasses and looked around the kitchen as if he'd never seen it before. That's how Dad tended to look at everything. He always seemed sort of—surprised. "So, when do we eat?" he asked.

"Just—about—now," said Molly, as she rushed from Dad back to the stove. She put the oven mitt back on and lifted the skillet off the heat. She stirred some soft butter into the thickening sauce, then looked frantically at the recipe again. "Oh! We forgot to chop up the parsley! I need to add it right now!"

"I'll do it," said Mom calmly, reaching for a knife.

"Oh! The rice!" cried Amanda. "Is it burning?"

Amanda rushed over to the pot and turned off the flame. She lifted the lid and stirred the rice with a wooden spoon. "I almost forgot about it," she admitted. "Uh-oh—there's a lot stuck to the bottom of the pan!"

Mom stood over Amanda. "It's okay, sweetie," she assured her. "It's a little overcooked on the bottom, that's all. The rest is perfect. Smell all those spices! I'll get you a bowl. Matthew, get the silverware, please. Molly, here's a big platter for the chicken. Now just give me a second to chop the parsley and add it to your sauce."

Molly and Amanda sighed with relief. They were glad Mom was home and taking charge now. Mom was a good cook. She usually cooked big breakfasts and dinners on the weekends. And she'd cook food on Sundays that the family could eat for at least part of the week. But lately, Mom had been working really hard, especially on the weekends. The twins knew Mom felt guilty about it, so they tried not to complain when they couldn't hang out with her as much.

Meanwhile, Dad had gone upstairs to the linen closet and found two silver candlesticks and a deep blue tablecloth with a gold-and-red design. In just a minute, Dad and Matthew made the table look like it belonged in a fancy restaurant.

"*MROW!*" howled Kitty desperately, running back and forth. Everyone laughed.

"Don't worry, Kitty," said Mom. "We'll let you have a piece, but I don't think you'll want it with the lemon sauce." She cut off a piece of chicken and put it on a saucer. "Here, Matthew, give this to Kitty."

Then Mom showed the twins how to arrange the chicken in a pretty way on the platter. In a few seconds, she'd laid each chicken breast slightly on top of the other. The chicken fanned out all the way across the platter.

"You'd better let me pour the sauce over the chicken," said Mom, reaching for the oven mitt. "This pan is heavy." As the twins watched, Mom slowly poured the lemony sauce on top of the chicken. The slices of lemon that had been cooked in the sauce added a nice yellow color to the golden chicken. And the green parsley brightened the dish and made it pretty.

"Wow!" said the twins. The plate looked like a photo in a cookbook.

"I can't believe we made that!" exclaimed Amanda as Mom ground some black pepper onto the chicken.

"I'm very impressed!" said Mom, smiling, as she brought the platter to the table.

"Me, too!" said Dad. "I guess you two are really growing up."

"Uh, remember? We haven't even tried it yet," said Matthew with an evil grin. Mom raised one eyebrow and shot him her "watch-it-kid-I'm-on-to-you" look. Matthew quickly added, "But *maybe* it'll be good."

"*Maybe!*" said Molly. "You're gonna be begging for more, Matthew!" She went to the fridge and pulled out the salad. "Bummer!" she cried. "The avocado looks kind of icky. It's not as green. And the lettuce is all wilted. Yuck!"

Matthew ran over to see the salad. "*Oooooh*, gross!" he said. "*I'm* not eating it."

Dad took the salad bowl from Molly and inspected it. "Don't worry, Molls," he said. "It won't affect the taste. Next time, just add the avocado and the salad dressing right before you serve it. That way, your lettuce will stay crispy, and the avocado will stay bright green."

"Okay," said Molly with a sigh, suddenly realizing that her legs were stiff from standing for so long. She ran upstairs to quickly change out of her flour-covered clothes. She threw on a T-shirt and Amanda's denim capris, then joined the family at the kitchen table. It felt good to sit down.

Dad looked around the table at everyone. "This is a special occasion!" he said, raising his glass of wine. "Everyone, lift your glass for a toast, please. Careful, Matthew."

Mom lifted her wineglass, and Matthew and the girls lifted their glasses of milk.

"To our chefs," said Dad. Molly smiled and felt her cheeks turn red. She turned to Amanda and saw that she was blushing, too. They'd never been toasted before.

Mom began to serve the chicken, and everyone passed the salad and the rice. Finally, after what seemed like ten hours, it was time to eat!

Mom was the first to try the chicken. She cut a neat piece of chicken and put it in her mouth.

"Well?" asked Molly.

"Um, how is it?" asked Amanda anxiously.

The twins waited for an answer. Was their meal going to be a success? Or one big, huge flop?

M om beamed.

"It's *great!* I love it! The chicken is so juicy, and I can really taste the lemon. That's because you cooked the lemon slices into the sauce, and the oils from the lemon rind added a lot of flavor," said Mom. "I'm so proud of you both! I couldn't have done a better job myself."

"Me neither," said Dad. "This is delicious, girls. The capers are a nice touch. They go well with the lemon. Where've I been? I didn't know you could cook."

"We didn't, either," said Amanda. "So, Matthew, what do you think?"

For once, Matthew didn't have anything to say. His mouth was too full of chicken, and the sauce was trickling down his chin. But he actually smiled at his big sisters and gave the "thumbs-up" sign.

Molly and Amanda looked at each other. "He likes it!" they cried. They finally dug into their own food.

"Wow! It really *is* good!" said Molly.

"Well, Molly, you got your chicken piccata," said Amanda. The twins took turns telling the family all about Molly's idea, finding the recipe online, shopping at the grocery store, and not knowing what capers were.

"Lots of people don't know what capers are," said Dad. "And now you do."

The twins looked at each other, their eyebrows raised. Once again, they were having the "twin thing." They'd both just realized that...

"Hey!" said Amanda. "We still don't know what they are."

Molly giggled and said, "We only know what they look like!"

"Well," said Mom, "capers are actually little pickles."

"Pickles!" said Dad. "Pickled what, exactly?" He whispered to Matthew, "I thought they were tiny little fish!"

"Capers are pickled flower buds of the caper shrub," replied Mom in her "teacher" voice. "The shrub grows in the Mediterranean region. So you see capers a lot in Italian, Greek, and Spanish food."

"You learn something new every day," said Daddy, crinkling his blue eyes at Mom. "Especially when you're married to a college professor. Pass the chicken, and the rice, please. And the salad."

There was a big mess to clean up afterward. The kitchen was full of the sounds of running water, the grinding garbage disposal, and clinking plates and glasses.

"This is the part about cooking I don't like," complained Molly, as she swept up the flour.

"It helps to clean as you go," said Mom as she wiped off the kitchen counter. "But that takes some practice! Listen, girls," she said in a serious voice. She cleared her throat.

Uh-oh, we're in for a lecture, thought Molly. She stood up.

Here it comes! thought Amanda.

"You should have called me and asked if you could have used the stove—and my knives!" continued Mom. "I'm glad you did such a great job, but you could have hurt yourselves. You know, I wouldn't have let you do this tonight without Dad or me here. I would have asked you to wait until we got home."

"Sorry," said Amanda, looking down at the floor.

"We just wanted it to be perfect," Molly tried to explain. "We wanted you to walk in the door and be surprised with a delicious dinner, like one in a restaurant!"

Mom couldn't help smiling then. "I was surprised, all right!" she said. "And it was as delicious as you wanted it to be. Thank you...just remember, in the future, you need to talk to me first about cooking."

"Okay," said the twins.

No one said anything for a moment. Then Amanda spoke up.

"I can't wait to tell Shawn that we're chefs now," she said, as she placed a dish in the dishwasher.

Shawn Jordan was Molly's and Amanda's best friend. She lived in an apartment building on Park Street, a few blocks away, with her dad. Molly and Amanda knew Shawn almost as well as they knew each other. The three were already good friends when Shawn's mom died a few years before, after a long illness. And since then, they'd gotten even closer.

Right now, Shawn was still in South Carolina, visiting her grandmother. The twins had missed her like anything. And Shawn missed them too. She'd sent them a long e-mail all about her funny Grandma Ruthie, and how her cousins Sonia and Jamal had taught her to ride a horse for the first time, and taken her to the beach.

"When is Shawn coming home?" asked Mom.

"Tomorrow!" replied the twins at the same time, giving each other a high-five.

"But we might not see her until the day after tomorrow," Amanda reminded Molly.

"Yeah, her dad's going to want to spend some time with her, too," said Molly.

Two long days later, Molly and Amanda were finally

sitting with Shawn in their favorite place in Park Terrace: Harry's. Harry's was the complete opposite of McDonald's. That's what was so great about it.

No chicken nuggets here. Harry's was a place you could go to get a wrap, a fruit smoothie, a pot of tea, slices of poppy-seed cake, or coffee (which always smelled great when it was brewing but tasted awful, thought the girls).

Harry's was actually an old drugstore, the type the girls' grandparents probably went to. It still had large, dark wooden cabinets with glass shelves and sliding-glass doors built into the walls. But the coolest thing was that all the dishes were one-of-a-kind, and old, and kind of wacky. If you ordered a pot of tea, you got it in a funky old teapot and none of the cups matched it. At home, that would be weird, maybe, but here, it looked cool, like all of the people who came into Harry's and stayed for hours as they sketched or wrote.

It had only been recently that the girls' parents would allow them to walk around Park Terrace without them. Park Terrace was a neighborhood in Brooklyn, New York, that bordered huge Prospect Park. It was across the river from Manhattan, just a subway ride away. The girls could explore all the cool pizzerias, bookstores, gift shops, and toy stores of Park Terrace, as long as they weren't alone. "The bigger the group, the better," said Mom.

Molly, Amanda, and Shawn had recently discovered Harry's, but it was kind of expensive, so they couldn't go there very often. It was a special event when they had enough allowance money to spend there. They felt a lot older than eleven when they sat at their own little table to have iced tea with mint, roasted-veggie wraps, lemon bars, or a pot of tea.

Shawn had been gone for just about three weeks, but she seemed different. Older. Maybe that was because she'd been to such a different place and tried new things. Shawn hadn't been into fashion much before, but now she was wearing lots of beaded bracelets on one arm. It felt a little strange to Molly and Amanda to see her at first. But that feeling only lasted until Shawn laughed and said, "Get outta here!" like she always did.

She'd gotten glasses, too, and they were the coolest. "Sonia and Jamal helped me pick them out," said Shawn. "Sonia said they're called cat glasses."

"I like them 'cause they're purple," said Amanda. "No one wears purple glasses!"

"Most kids wouldn't look good in those glasses," said Molly. "But you look amazing!"

"Thanks," said Shawn. "I got a couple of other pairs, too. They were running this *huge* sale. They're like wearing a bracelet or a hair band. They're my new fashion accessory!" The girls laughed.

Shawn had lots of photos from her trip to show the twins. "This is my cousin Jamal," said Shawn. "He drove me everywhere in his Jeep. And this is Grandma Ruthie. She looks mad because she didn't want me to take her picture, so I sneaked it! And here's me horseback riding...and with some kids we met at the beach...That's Sonia with me at my farewell pizza party. Doesn't she look like a model?"

Then it was the twins' turn to tell Shawn everything, though there wasn't much to report. But they made her laugh when they told her about Amanda's "furry chicken."

"...and so everybody liked our dinner!" Molly said.

"And we didn't even get salmonella poisoning," joked Amanda.

"I did some cooking this summer, too!" said Shawn. "My grandma showed me how to make biscuits from scratch. And she let me fry some catfish on top of the stove. We made cookies, too...hey, do you guys want to ride bikes in the park now?"

"Okay," replied Amanda as she finished the last bite of her grilled veggie wrap.

"We'll go get our bikes and meet you at your house," suggested Molly. "See you in a little while."

"Let's walk up a different street to go home," Amanda told Molly after they'd waved good-bye to Shawn. "We always go down Third Street. Let's go down Fifth Street instead."

As the twins walked down Fifth Street, they passed Park Terrace Cookware. And that's when they saw it: a big sign, with red lettering, that said:

KIDS!

Learn to cook, bake, make pastry! Classes start next week - inquire within.

4

"No way!" cried Molly. She stopped walking to stare at the sign.

"*Mmmm,* pastry," said Amanda dreamily.

"I'd love to take cooking classes," said Molly. "Wouldn't you, Manda?"

"Sure!" said Amanda. "Do you think Mom and Dad would let us?"

Molly checked out the smaller print on the sign. "Only eight dollars a class," she read, and turned to Amanda. "Do you think Shawn would take it with us?"

The twins couldn't wait to ask her, so they hurried home. Molly picked up the phone in the kitchen, where Kitty was busy clawing at her cardboard scratch pad. Amanda brought the cordless in from the den.

"Kitty, keep it down," called Molly as Shawn's phone rang. Kitty's sharp claws sure could make a racket on that cardboard.

"Hello? Jordan residence," said Shawn. Shawn's dad made her answer the phone that way. The twins knew it made Shawn felt like a geek, so they always giggled when they heard her say it. They were glad they didn't have to answer their phone like that.

"Agent Jordan?" said Molly in her secret-agent voice. "This is Agent Moore 001 and Agent Moore 002."

"Hi!" said Shawn. "Aren't you coming over?"

"Yeah," said Amanda, "but we have something very important to talk to you about. So important that it can't wait!"

"*What?*" cried Shawn.

"Cooking classes," replied the twins together.

"For kids!" said Molly.

"Only eight bucks a class," added Amanda. "You can learn to cook, bake, and make pastry!"

"Wow," said Shawn. "Do you think we'd get to wear those cool chef's hats? I could learn how to make my dad a birthday cake."

"And we could eat a lot of cake," giggled Amanda. "'Cause I'll bet they let you eat the food that you make in the class." Molly and Shawn laughed. Amanda could really pound the sugar!

"Cooking classes could be fun," said Shawn. "Especially because I just got back from South Carolina and I'm bored already!" She giggled. "Uh—no offense, guys."

"We know what you mean!" Molly assured her. "We're bored, too. That's mostly why we decided to cook a gourmet dinner for our whole family!"

"I'll ask my dad about it tonight," said Shawn. "He'll probably think it's cool. He's always trying to get me to try new things and not watch TV."

"TV! I remember TV," said Molly sadly. Their TV was broken and Mom and Dad didn't seem to be in any hurry to get it fixed.

"Great!" said Amanda. "We're going to take cooking classes together. If our parents say we can. And we're going to become *fab*-ulous chefs!"

"We'll have our own TV show!" added Molly.

"Yeah—we'll call it—Chef Girls!" giggled Shawn.

"Okay, Shawn, we're on our way over," said Amanda. "We'll meet you outside your building. Don't forget your bike helmet."

Amanda and Molly couldn't wait for their parents to get home from work so they could tell them all about the cooking classes.

"Let's bring it up after dinner," Amanda suggested when they biked home from the park. The girls had learned that when they asked Mom and Dad for things right when they came home from work and were tired and hungry, they were always told, "We'll discuss it after dinner" or, simply, "NO."

Mom got home first, and had several bags of groceries with her—"For my poor starving children," she said as she kissed Matthew, who was feeding Kitty, and Molly and Amanda, who were playing Scrabble at the kitchen table. As the girls helped put the groceries away, Mom said, "I'm sorry there wasn't much in the fridge to eat yesterday, girls. And I'm sorry we've had so much takeout and pizza lately...I've been working too much and neglecting you."

"Are we getting a *pizza?*" asked Matthew, his face lighting up.

"Matthew's not sick of takeout!" said Amanda, laughing. "It's just us, I guess!"

"Well, I'm tired of it, too," said Mom. "So I'm going to put on some shorts, and then we'll make some dinner."

"What are we having, Mom?" asked Matthew. He was holding Kitty awkwardly in his arms. She didn't look at all comfortable, but for some weird reason, she always put up with Matthew.

"I thawed some thick tuna steaks that your dad brought home from his fishing trip," replied Mom. "He'll grill them when he gets home. We'll finish off the rice you made the other day. And look at these gorgeous

42

tomatoes! They're so ripe. They'll be great with some fresh mozzarella."

"Yum!" cried Molly. She loved tomatoes and sliced mozzarella together.

"Can we eat outside tonight, Mom?" asked Amanda. The Moores had a long, narrow backyard, with a high wooden fence around it. It wasn't a yard, really, but it had a patio, a flower garden, a large tree, a few lawn chairs, and even a picnic table.

"We'll eat in the garden if you and Molly wipe off the table out there and bring out everything we'll need," replied Mom, as she left the kitchen to change her clothes.

"Okay," said the twins. They loved to eat in the garden. So while Mom sliced the tomatoes and fresh mozzarella, they brought all the chairs, place mats, dishes, silverware, and glasses outside.

"We can't forget the citronella candles," said Amanda, "to keep away the mosquitoes."

"Hi, everyone!" Dad's voice suddenly boomed from the hallway. He appeared in the kitchen. "Hi, honey! Hi, kids! What's going on?"

"You're grilling tuna steaks!" Mom told him.

"Sounds good to me!"

After dinner, as everyone was sitting around the table listening to the crickets, Molly and Amanda were just about to bring up the subject of the cooking classes when Dad said, "Oh! I forgot something. I'll be right back." He went inside.

A few minutes later, he came out with a large brown paper bag and said, "Molly and Amanda, close your eyes, and you will get a big surprise."

The twins looked at each other. What could it be? It wasn't their birthday.

"Okay, they're closed," said Molly, closing her eyes tightly and holding out her hand.

"Mine, too," said Amanda.

Dad put something light and crumpled in each of the girls' hands. They opened their eyes to find...

"Chefs' hats!" exclaimed the twins.

"Cool!" said Matthew, even though the gift wasn't for him.

"Actually, a chef's hat is called a *toque blanche*," said Dad. "I just learned that today. They're for you, our budding chefs!"

"Thanks, Dad," said the girls.

"You're welcome," he said, "but wait! There's more!"

"What else?" asked the twins.

"Well, I was walking from the subway down Fifth

44

Street, and I passed Park Terrace Cookware, so I went in. That's where I found your hats. And it turns out that they're offering cooking classes for kids. What a coincidence, huh?"

The twins' eyes opened wide. Amanda and Molly glanced at each other and tried not to laugh.

"So, how about it, girls? Wouldn't you like to take those classes?" asked Dad.

"I think you should take those classes," added Mom. "I'd feel a lot better if you did."

"Why?" Amanda wanted to know.

"You'd learn how to do things safely in a kitchen," Mom replied. "And you'd learn how to use a knife correctly, too. I hate to think how you could have hurt yourselves the other night with my sharp knives!"

"Um, we have something to tell you," announced Molly.

"What?" asked Mom and Dad.

"*We* were going to ask *you* if we could take those cooking classes!" blurted Amanda, laughing.

"Yeah! We were hoping you'd let us, and we didn't think you'd be practically *telling* us to take them," added Molly. "We thought we could pay for the classes out of our allowance."

"No, no," Dad told the twins. "Mom and I know you would like to have gone to camp this summer, and we aren't taking a big family vacation because of all the work we had done on the house. Matthew just got his new bike, and this is our gift to you."

"Thank you," said the twins together. Mom and Dad smiled.

"We'll sign you up tomorrow," promised Mom.

On the first day of cooking class, Molly and Amanda went to pick up Shawn. Molly was wearing denim capris and a baby-blue T-shirt that said "Brooklyn" on it. Amanda was decked out in an orange tank top with embroidered flowers on it and khaki cargo pants. She'd put glitter in her hair. Both girls wore sneakers, but they couldn't have looked more different: Molly wore canvas low-tops in pine green, and Amanda wore high-tech slip-ons with plastic webbing on the front.

"Hi, guys," said Shawn when she opened the door of her apartment. She was wearing a short black T-shirt, lime-green capris with embroidery along the hem, and black wedge sandals. *Shawn always looks so together,* thought Molly.

Amanda pointed at Shawn's sandals, saying, "We aren't allowed to wear sandals, remember?"

"*Oops!*" exclaimed Shawn. "I forgot: 'no open-toed shoes.'" This was for safety reasons, in case something hot spilled, or a knife fell to the floor.

46

"Come on in," said Shawn. "I'll change my shoes and then we can go."

Molly went straight for the window, which she always did when she went to Shawn's. It had an awesome view of the meadows and woods of Prospect Park, which was one of New York's largest parks. She could see tiny people jogging, playing baseball, and just relaxing on the grass. Beyond that she could see some of the lake, where turtles and swans and ducks lived.

Amanda was checking out a wooden giraffe that was taller than she was. Mr. and Mrs. Jordan had brought it back from the country of Zimbabwe, in Africa. Before they'd had Shawn, they'd visited Africa a few times and brought back lots of cool things: rugs, baskets, tribal masks, and wooden animals.

"Okay!" said Shawn, who was now wearing bright white sneakers. "I'm ready to go!"

The girls were half a block away from Park Terrace Cookware, when Amanda suddenly said, "Uh-oh."

"What?" asked Molly and Shawn quickly.

"Look who's going into the store," whispered Amanda. She pointed to a tall girl with chin-length blonde hair. "Natasha Ross!"

"Natasha *Ross*! No way!" shouted Molly.

Amanda flashed Molly "the look."

"I mean, Natasha Ross, no way," Molly repeated in a loud whisper.

"Do you think she's taking the class, too?" asked Shawn.

"I'll bet she is," replied Molly and Amanda at the same time. They watched Natasha wave good-bye to her mother and go into the store.

"Oh, *no*," groaned the girls all at once. This could change everything.

None of them were in the mood for Natasha Ross.

After a moment, Shawn shrugged. "Well, let's keep going," she said. "I don't want to be late."

"Yeah, we can't let Natasha keep us from taking our class," added Molly. But her throat felt tight and her toes curled inside her sneakers.

"O-kay," said Amanda. She was nervously snapping and unsnapping a pocket of her cargo pants.

The girls walked in silence the rest of the way to the store, but they were all thinking about the same thing: how Natasha had once told the principal that Amanda and Molly cheated on an important science test. The story was whispered over and over again around the school. And when Shawn explained to everyone that Natasha had lied, Natasha spread another rumor that Shawn had cheated, too.

"Are you here for the cooking class?" asked a gray-haired man in a store apron as the girls walked in the door.

"Yes," said the girls.

"Go right to the back," said the man. "That's where the class is."

"Okay, thank you," said Shawn.

The girls headed through the store. From floor to ceiling, it was crammed with cookware. Shiny pots and pans of every size. Muffin tins. Blenders. Food processors. Heavy roasting pans. Cake pans. Bread pans of all different sizes. There were also colorful napkins, place mats, tablecloths, and dishes. One entire wall held little gadgets such as potato peelers, brushes for cleaning vegetables, and garlic presses.

In the back room was a kitchen so clean that it sparkled. Two rows of long tables, each with wooden tops and chrome legs, lined the center of the room. They held cutting boards, butter, one wet dish towel, one dry dish towel, and containers of kosher salt for each student. And in the middle of each table, there were a few pepper mills and bottles of olive oil for the students to share.

Around the sides of the kitchen were a large refrigerator, two gigantic stoves with hoods on top, and two big sinks. There was a pantry with lots of spices and glass containers full of pasta, beans, and rice. There was even a small washing machine and a dryer.

Kids were leaning against the tables, talking to one

another or just looking around. The girls knew some of them.

"There's David Stern," said Shawn, spotting a serious-looking boy with glasses. He was staring at the spice rack.

"Hey! Peichi's here!" exclaimed Molly. "Hi, Peichi." Molly waved at a girl who had long, shiny black hair pulled back with a headband. The twins had known Peichi Cheng since kindergarten.

And, of course, there was Natasha, looking right at Molly, Amanda, and Shawn. Natasha was standing at the end of the first table, which the girls had to pass by. *Just my luck*, thought Amanda, who was closest to Natasha.

"Hi," mumbled Amanda, trying to sound casual. She had to say something. She watched Molly and Shawn walk away and find places at a table. *How could they leave me alone like this?* she thought.

"Oh, hi, Molly," said Natasha, sounding bored. Her eyes were a cold blue color.

"It's Amanda," replied Amanda.

"Oh, right," said Natasha, shrugging her shoulders. "Whatever. What are you doing here?"

"The same thing as you are, I guess," retorted Amanda as she kept walking. Her cheeks were burning as she passed Molly. "Thanks a lot, Molly!" she said under her breath.

"Sorry, Manda," said Molly. "But there were people behind us. We had to keep moving." Molly's table was full, so she motioned for Amanda to stand behind her at the back table.

Amanda didn't have time to dwell on Natasha, because a young woman walked in and stood at the front of the class. She was wearing her reddish-blond hair in a ponytail and a chef's apron over her pants and shirt. She was joined by a young man with short dark hair and a goatee. He was wearing a chef's apron, too.

"Hello, everyone!" the woman said with a big smile. Her brown eyes looked friendly. "My name is Carmen Piccolo, and I'll be your cooking instructor. This is Freddie Gonzalez, my assistant. Welcome to class! You're going to learn a lot. And when the course is finished, you'll get a graduation present. See the chefs' aprons that Freddie is passing out? When you complete this course, Park Terrace Cookware will embroider your name on your apron, and you'll get to keep it!"

"Cool!" said a few kids.

"Now," Carmen announced, "We have a lot to do today. We're going to make carrot soup with fresh ginger, fresh pasta with a fresh tomato sauce, roast chicken with a mushroom sauce, a salad with our own dressing, and for dessert, an apple crisp."

"Wow!" cried Peichi, who stood at the front table. "Do we get to eat it all, too?" Everyone laughed.

"You bet!" said Carmen with a chuckle. "'Cause Freddie and I can't eat it all by ourselves!" Everyone laughed again.

"Each work station has two dish towels," continued Carmen, "because, in a real restaurant kitchen, a chef uses the wet one for cleaning around the work station—and the dry one as a pot holder."

Carmen smiled again as she looked around at all the students. "Are you ready to get started?" she asked.

"Yeah!" shouted the class.

"Great!" exclaimed Carmen. "First, I'm going to show you some very important things you need to know starting with some knife skills."

"Oooooh!" cried all the boys.

Carmen ignored them.

"This is a chef's knife," she said, picking up a large, pointy knife.

"Bring out the Band-Aids!" called one kid in the back row.

"Ver-r-r-y scar-y!" cracked his buddy, trying to sound like Dracula.

Carmen looked up. "It's not scary if you know how to use it correctly," she said. "And this," she added, picking up a very small knife with a wooden handle, "is a paring knife. We'll be using both of these knives today. Oh, I have a few safety issues to talk about, too. Everyone, please lift up your cutting boards."

The kids looked at each other, puzzled. Why would she want them to do that, they wondered.

"You'll see that under each cutting board is a wet paper towel," said Carmen. "That's to keep your cutting board from slipping as you're cutting, which would be very dangerous! I want you to always do this when you're using knives in your kitchens at home. And *never* use knives without your parents' permission. Okay?"

"Okay," answered the class.

"Which do you think is safer to work with—a sharp knife or a dull knife?" asked Carmen.

"A dull knife?" answered some kids, including Amanda. Molly wasn't sure.

"It's actually a sharp knife," replied Carmen. "That's because a dull blade could drag and slip when you're cutting with it, and could cut the fingers on your other hand. But a sharp blade cuts quickly and cleanly. It helps you work more efficiently. One more thing," said

Carmen. "You will not walk around this class with a knife. Get it?"

"Got it!" answered the class.

"However, if you're at home, and you have a big kitchen, and you have to walk a little way with a knife—or if you're handing the knife to someone—always hold it with the knifepoint pointing towards the floor. Your hand should be gripping the handle. Get it?"

"Got it!"

"Good!" said Carmen. "Now I'm going to show you how to slice." She pulled a potato from a basket of vegetables. "The fingertips of the hand that is *not* using the knife should be curled down so that only the flat part of the knuckle is facing the blade. This way, your fingertips are away from the blade and they won't get cut."

Carmen sliced through the potato from the tip of the knife to the bottom end. Then she guided her knife back up again in a rocking motion to the tip. She quickly sliced through the potato with the rocking motion. "Freddie's bringing around knives and vegetables to practice on," she told the class. "Now you try. Just try the motion of slicing first, and then practice with a potato or zucchini."

At first it felt awkward for Molly to curl her fingers under while her other hand sliced with the rocking motion. It all felt so slow, while Carmen make it look so quick and easy.

"How's it going, Molls?" called Amanda.

"Not so well," replied Molly, without looking up from her potato. She gripped the knife so hard that her hand began to cramp. Carmen was now walking around to watch everyone, and she stopped at Molly.

"There's no need to work so hard," Carmen told her. "Your knife is sharp. Let it do the work."

But Amanda caught on quickly, and Carmen noticed.

"She's got it," announced Carmen to the class. "What's your name, please?"

"Amanda," said Amanda, blushing.

"Amanda is making this look easy and relaxed," said Carmen. "Keep going, Amanda, I want everyone to see. Here's another potato. Amanda is letting the knife blade do the work. And do you see how she's continuing to move her fingertips away from the blade while moving the potato toward the knife? Excellent, Amanda. The key is to feel that the blade never really lifts from the cutting board."

Carmen moved on to showing how to use a paring knife. The kids practiced using a paring knife on the apples that would be used for the dessert.

"Now," said Carmen, "I'm going to split you into small groups of three. Each group will make part of the dinner.

Some will make the carrot soup, some will work on the chicken dish, and so on. Now count off in threes, starting with you." She pointed to Peichi. "You're a 'one,'" Carmen told her. "The 'ones' will make the chicken dish."

Everyone counted off. It turned out that Shawn and Amanda ended up being "threes" together. They were in the carrot soup and apple crisp group.

Molly was a "one."

Don't be a "one," Natasha, don't be a "one," Molly was hoping as the group at Natasha's table counted off.

"One," said Natasha.

That's just great, thought Molly. *Well, at least Peichi is in my group, too.*

"So—we're the chicken-with-mushroom-sauce gang!" said Molly when she joined Peichi and Natasha at their table. She forced herself to smile.

Natasha smirked at no one in particular. When she finally looked at Molly, Molly felt as though Natasha's cold blue eyes were looking right through her. *Anybody in there?* thought Molly. *She's giving me the creeps!*

Luckily, Peichi was able to fill up the silence. "The chicken sounds good, huh?" she asked. "This is gonna be fun! I love to cook! I mean, I haven't really cooked before, but I love to bake cookies and sometimes I help my dad when he cooks. Do you ever do that? I love baking brownies, don't you? Do you ever make homemade brownies? My dad does. They're great! I like Carmen, don't you? She's great!"

Thank you, Peichi, thought Molly, as she nodded "yes" to all of Peichi's questions. Molly had never known Peichi to be anything other than enthusiastic—about everything! Peichi didn't even seem to notice that Natasha was looking right through her, too. Or maybe she just didn't care!

Freddie approached their table. It was his job to bring around everything that each group needed.

After he learned the girls' names, he asked. "You're doing the chicken, right?"

"Right!" they all replied.

"Ladies, your chicken awaits!" said Freddie dramatically, as he brought out a bundle wrapped in brown paper. "Say hello!" With that, he unwrapped the paper.

There on the table was a whole chicken, although it was missing a few things: its feathers and its head.

"*Eeewwwww!*" cried Molly and Natasha together.

"It's—a dead—thing!" added Molly. Everyone heard the girls, and looked over to see the chicken.

"*Eeewwwww!*" shouted the rest of the class.

But Peichi just laughed.

"You've never seen a whole dead chicken before?" she asked Molly and Natasha.

"Have you, Peichi?" asked Freddie.

"Yeah, all the time! My grandparents have a grocery store in Chinatown!"

"In the Manhattan Chinatown, or the Brooklyn Chinatown?" asked Freddie.

"Manhattan," replied Peichi. "They hang them in the store windows, only they're cooked! Ducks, too."

"That's right," said Freddie.

Carmen asked the class to watch Freddie. "He's going to show you how to truss the chicken," said Carmen. "That means to tie its legs back against its body. This will make it easier to handle, because the legs, wing, and neck skin will stay in one place. Plus it will just look better when you serve it."

Freddie unwrapped a long piece of string, cut it, and put it under the rear end of the bird. Then he looped the string around the ends of the legs, crossed it over the breast, looped it under and around the wings, and knotted it on top of the bird.

"Ta-da!" announced Freddie.

"Ouch!" called one of the wisecracking boys.

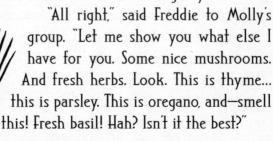

"All right," said Freddie to Molly's group. "Let me show you what else I have for you. Some nice mushrooms. And fresh herbs. Look. This is thyme... this is parsley. This is oregano, and—smell this! Fresh basil! Hah? Isn't it the best?"

"Mmmm," said all three girls as they breathed in the smell of the green basil leaves.

"You guys have a big job, because you're cooking the main course! I guess that means you're special, huh? Well, I have a secret for you." Freddie began to whisper in a loud, funny way. "It's really, really easy to do!" He smiled. "And I'm gonna tell you a secret of French cooking. The trick with most meats and fish is to start cooking them on top of the stove, and finish them in the oven."

Molly spoke up. "So you mean, we won't have it in the oven the whole time? We'll put it in a pan first? This whole bird?"

"Well, duh! That's what he just said," Natasha told Molly sarcastically. Freddie and Peichi looked at Natasha, startled that she would say something like that. Molly's cheeks burned. She looked down at her cutting board.

"Er—right, exactly, we'll put it in a skillet first," Freddie told Molly. "It helps keep the meat moist. There's nothing worse than dried-out chicken. Right? Now let's preheat the oven to five hundred degrees." He smiled and nodded reassuringly at Molly as if to say, *Don't let Natasha bother you!*

Peichi sneaked Molly a little smile. Molly tried to smile back. She suddenly gulped in air, realizing that she'd been holding her breath without knowing it.

60

"Molly, why don't you salt and pepper the chicken?" Freddie suggested. "Natasha and Peichi, you can start chopping the herbs."

Molly shot Freddie a look that said, *Thank you for separating me from Natasha.*

CLANG! CRASH!

"Aaghh!" shouted some kids, startled by the sudden noise.

A copper pot and its lid had dropped to the floor.

Right by Natasha.

Natasha had accidentally knocked them off the table when she'd turned around to see what the salad group was doing.

Natasha's neck turned red, and the color rose into her chin and up into her cheeks like the mercury in a thermometer.

"Good going, Molly," Natasha called out. The pot and lid remained on the floor.

"Wha—what?" gasped Molly. "I didn't do anything!"

A few of the boys laughed. Then the kitchen went silent.

Molly couldn't see. Everything was a blur, like when she tried on Dad's glasses. Where was Amanda?

"No harm done," said Freddie, who was nearby. "The pot was empty." He glanced at Natasha. He could tell that she wasn't about to pick it up, so he did it himself.

Molly's eyes refocused and found Amanda across the

kitchen at the sink. Amanda's eyes said to Molly, *Here I am. You're okay.*

If you say so, Molly's eyes replied.

Carmen cleared her throat.

"Well!" she said brightly. "Let's keep going—you're all doing so well!"

"Okay, folks, move along, nothing to see here," joked Freddie as he placed the pot and lid back on the table.

The kids turned back into their tables and started talking and measuring and chopping again.

Shawn happened to be nearby, so she casually approached Molly's table. Shawn was so cool that she made it look as though she was borrowing some olive oil from Molly, but she was actually asking, in her low, calm voice, "Do you want to take a break? Outside?"

Molly shook her head no and looked down. Suddenly she felt like she was going to cry.

Shawn knew what to do. She knew that Molly would die if anyone knew she was upset. So Shawn walked back to her work station, cool and casual, so that Molly could pretend she was all right—and not let Natasha win.

chapter

6

Freddie helped Molly, Peichi, and Natasha as they chopped the herbs, some of which they put inside the chicken. Then they heated olive oil and a little butter together in a big skillet and put the chicken in to brown. Freddie held the chicken down gently with a big chef's fork.

"We'll brown it for just about a minute on each side," said Freddie. "That'll give it a nice color. Then we'll pop it in the oven!"

"Do we have to take it out of the skillet and put it in a different dish for the oven?" asked Peichi.

"I'll put it on a rack in a pan," said Freddie. "Then we'll baste it with the rest of the herbs, salt, pepper, and olive oil."

"That *is* easy!" said Molly. She felt better now. *I'm just going to have to ignore Natasha,* she told herself.

"So, while the chicken's browning, why don't you all start dicing the mushrooms for the sauce," Freddie told the girls. "I'm gonna check on the pasta group over there, and I'll be back later."

"Okay!" said Molly and Peichi. Natasha nodded. Sort of.

As soon as Freddie walked away, Natasha moved the bowl of mushrooms near herself so that Molly and Peichi couldn't reach any. She began to dice them.

"Um, we'll take some, too," said Peichi.

"Yeah, then we can all help," added Molly, her voice shaking. *What was Natasha's deal?*

Natasha didn't look up or move the bowl. Peichi shot Molly a glance that said, *Can you believe this?* Then Peichi just reached over and pushed the bowl into the middle of the table. Molly smiled at Peichi, and Natasha saw it.

"Watch it, Molly," she said between her teeth. "Or I'll tell Carmen."

Molly and Peichi looked at each other and began to laugh nervously.

"Tell her what?" Molly asked Natasha.

Natasha stared back. Then she said, "I'll tell her that you guys aren't giving me a chance to do anything."

"Well," said Peichi, who for once was not smiling, "That would be a lie, wouldn't it?" Natasha didn't say anything.

Molly didn't say anything, either, though she was

grateful to Peichi for sticking up for her. By now Molly just wanted to get through the class. She'd given up on having a lot of fun.

Molly sighed and looked over at Amanda's and Shawn's table. Their group was laughing and talking. *They* were getting along as they cooked carrots, celery, garlic, and an onion in chicken stock to make the base for the soup.

About an hour later, class was rocking.

By then the pasta group, which turned out to have all boys in it, had gotten too rowdy.

Carmen made a time-out signal with her hands, and called out, "Girls, listen up!" She looked right at Molly. "Who would like to switch groups with one of the pasta boys?"

Molly's hand went up like a shot. "I will!" she practically shouted. Across the room, Freddie smiled at her.

"See ya later, Peichi," whispered Molly as she left the table. "Um, thanks for, you know."

"Don't forget to write!" joked Peichi.

Natasha, of course, looked the other way and didn't say anything.

"Guys, say hi to Molly," ordered Carmen.

"Hi," said the boys, rolling their eyes at each other. They looked bummed out to lose one of their guys and inherit a girl.

Whatever, thought Molly. *They've got to be better than Natasha, anyway.*

"So, what are we doing?" asked Molly.

Carmen patted some dough that was sitting on a cutting board. "We've just made the dough for the pasta," she explained. "It's very simple. All it takes is semolina flour, salt, and eggs. The flour and salt are combined in a little mound, and the eggs go in the middle of that. Each of the guys took a turn kneading the dough. See how it's slightly sticky? That's good."

Carmen looked up at the group. "Okay," she said. "We're going to cut the pasta now." She clamped a metal pasta-rolling machine to the counter. Then she sprinkled the work surface with flour. She gave Molly and the

other kids each some dough, and wrapped the rest of it in plastic wrap so that it wouldn't dry out.

"Now roll the dough in flour, not too much, and flatten it a little," she said, showing them. Then she cranked the dough through the machine. Out came a wide strip of flattened dough. She passed it back through the machine several times, and when she was finished, she had long, thin strips of pasta.

It was fun to make the pasta. Everyone took turns doing two things: cranking the pasta machine to make the strips of pasta come out, and holding the pasta strips to keep them from breaking as they came through the machine.

The sauce was quick to make, so the group didn't make it until shortly before it was time to eat. Carmen showed how to core a tomato by cutting a wedge around the core, then just taking it out. Then she cut an "X" into the bottom of the tomato. "Now everyone try," she said.

Once everyone had prepared their tomatoes, they put them in boiling water.

"We'll keep them in there for only thirty seconds," said Carmen. "This is to loosen the skins. Then we'll put them under cold water, which will make it easier to take the skins off. Skins and seeds can sometimes taste bitter."

Next, she showed how to remove the seeds. She cut the tomatoes in half and squeezed out the seeds and liquid into a strainer that was set over a bowl. "We'll keep the liquid," she said. "Now all we do is crush the tomatoes, cook them in the olive oil and garlic that we are heating, add the tomato liquid, salt, pepper, and basil, and soon it will be a delicious sauce!"

Amanda's and Shawn's group thought making the carrot soup was easy. After they'd boiled down the carrots, celery, garlic and onion, Carmen brought out a tool called a hand blender. "I love this thing," she said, as she held it in the pot and turned it on. It quickly blended the vegetables into a thick liquid called a purée. "And now we'll add the fresh ginger, and that's it! Carrot soup!"

Finally it was time to eat everything. As the class watched, Freddie carved the chicken.

"Yo, I'm starving!" said a kid named Thomas.

"Then help me get all the food out to the table, man," said Freddie.

Thomas, Amanda, and Shawn helped Freddie bring the plates of food out to a big table in a room behind the kitchen. The table had been set earlier with a tablecloth, pretty plates and glasses, and even cloth napkins.

Everyone sat down. Molly, Amanda, Shawn, and Peichi sat next to each other. Shawn and Amanda were the first ones to remember to put their napkins on their laps. Everyone copied them.

"Go ahead and start," Carmen told the class as she took off her apron. "Freddie and I will join you in a minute."

Suddenly, everyone became quiet as they passed the food around. Everyone felt kind of shy eating together at the big table.

Then Peichi tried the carrot soup and exclaimed, "Wow! This is *great!*"

Everyone laughed.

Pretty soon everyone was eating and talking and laughing.

"We *rocked* when we made this salad!"

"Hey, don't you wish the school cafeteria was like this?"

"The chicken is really juicy!"

"Pass the mushroom sauce!"

"Yo, man, say please!"

"That was fun!" exclaimed Shawn as the girls walked out of Park Terrace Cookware.

"Except for the Natasha part," Molly pointed out.

"I hope she isn't in my group next time," said Amanda.

"I'm not going to let Natasha spoil class for *me*," declared Shawn. She stopped walking and put her hands on her hips. "Even if she is in my group. Who cares? It's my class, too, and *I'm* gonna have fun."

The twins' eyes opened wide. "You're right!" said Molly.

"You go, Shawn," added Amanda. "So what do you want to do now? Get some ice cream from the Mr. Freezy truck?" She looked longingly at the big blue truck that had a picture of a man made out of an ice-cream cone. Carnival music from the truck echoed through the street.

"How can you eat again?" shrieked Shawn.

"Let's just go home and have something cold to drink," suggested Molly. "It's really hot out here. We don't have any money, anyway, Amanda. You coming, Shawn?"

"No, I can't," said Shawn. "I have to baby-sit a kid in my building, and then I have to do my summer reading."

"We have to do our summer reading, too," Amanda said, looking at Molly. "Actually, Molly does. I've finished all my required summer reading." Amanda loved to read.

"Goody two-shoes for you, Princess," retorted Molly. "I have plenty of time to finish my summer reading." Molly rarely read anything that wasn't required of her in school.

"I'll call you tomorrow," said Shawn with a wave. "'Bye."

"Call us tonight," said Molly, "because we're going to our grandpa's house tomorrow, for the weekend."

"Oh, yeah!" exclaimed Shawn. "I forgot! Lucky you— I wish I were going to the beach this weekend."

Molly and Amanda walked home, past the Mr. Freezy truck, down shady, tree-lined Third Street with its tall, one hundred year-old townhouses, across Seventh Avenue and past their favorite pizza parlor.

They couldn't wait to tell Mom about their class.

But she was busy with Matthew, listening to him practice his violin, which they could hear screeching outside before they even reached the house. So the twins hung out in the garden, which was shady and cool. Molly finally started her required reading, and Amanda read a mystery book that she'd borrowed from Shawn.

"Hi! You're home!" called Mom later, from the kitchen window.

She came outside and brought three glasses of lemonade with her. She was wearing her new outfit that the girls had picked out: a black-and-white polka-dotted halter top with flared white capris.

"So, how was it?" she asked. "What did you make?"

"What *didn't* we make, is the question," Amanda replied with a laugh. "We made a huge meal! It was great!"

"What about you, Molls? Didn't you have fun?" asked Mom.

"It was fun, but it could've been a lot funner," answered Molly.

"You mean *more fun*, not funner," said Mom.

Molly sighed impatiently. "Okay, more fun."

Mom nestled into the chaise lounge. "So, tell me all about it. What happened? Didn't your dish turn out well?"

"Yeah, it turned out. It was delicious, actually. Mushroom sauce is really easy to make."

"Oh. Didn't you like the teacher?"

Molly didn't answer, so Amanda spoke up. "Natasha was in Molly's chicken-with-mushroom-sauce group," she explained.

Mom sat forward in her chair. "You mean Natasha Ross? The one that gave you all that trouble last year?"

"Yup, the one and only," replied Molly.

"So what happened?" asked Mom.

"She was mean to me in front of Peichi, and Freddie, the assistant! She dropped a pot on the floor and it made a loud noise and then she said *I* did it! She hogged the mushrooms and then said she'd tell our teacher that I wasn't letting her work on them, even though it wasn't even *true*! She's a big fat liar and she's so incredibly mean and I don't know *why*!" ranted Molly.

"She was pretty rude to me, too, Mom," added Amanda.

"Oh," said Mom. She set her glass down on the table.

"Mom," said Amanda, "Why *is* Natasha so mean to us? We never did anything to her. Really!"

Mom sighed. "I don't know why Natasha is mean to you," she replied. "Maybe she's a very unhappy girl. We don't know what her home life is like. Maybe she's angry about something, and she needs someone to take it out on."

"Why us?" asked Molly. "What did *we* ever do to *her*?"

"What should we do about it?" asked Amanda.

Mom smiled and said, "Be as nice to her as you can."

Molly's jaw dropped. "What for?" she asked.

"Look, girls," began Mom. "This world already has a

lot of hatred in it. I want you both to be as forgiving as possible. I want you to accept people the way they are. I know that Natasha isn't your favorite person. But I don't want you to be mean to Natasha or to feel that you need to get back at her."

"*Hmmm,*" said Molly. She wasn't so sure.

"I want you to promise me that the next time you see her, you'll smile at her and say hi," added Mom. "That's all. You might be surprised—maybe she'll be nice to *you*."

"And what if she isn't?" asked Amanda.

"At least you'll know that you did all you could. Okay? Will you do that for me?"

"Okay," replied the twins in a mopey voice.

"But that's gonna be hard, Mom," added Molly. "'Cause I'm really mad."

"I know," stated Mom, nodding her head.

That night, Molly asked, "Amanda? Are you asleep?"

"*Mmmpphh,*" was Amanda's reply from her bed across the twin's big room.

"I can't sleep. I'm still so *mad* at Natasha. How could she do that to me?"

"*I-da-knowpphh.*"

"What did you think of what Mom said today?"

Molly asked. "About Natasha? I mean, I guess she's right. But maybe Natasha just *likes* to be mean."

"*Mmmmm.*"

Molly stared up at the ceiling that had glow-in-the-dark stars on it. "Hey, Amanda? Are you nervous about starting middle school in September? We're gonna be the low girls on the totem pole again...Amanda?"

Amanda was sound asleep.

Molly turned onto her side and watched the night sky through the large window, the one above the cushioned window seat. She saw a plane climb high into the sky and thought about gigantic Windsor Middle School with sixth-, seventh-, and eighth-graders. Long, winding halls crowded with faces...so many classrooms...so many stairs...

Molly slept.

chapter 8

The next morning was Saturday, the day the Moores were going to the New Jersey shore to visit Poppy. Molly was awakened by the thumping sounds of Matthew hopping, running, and jumping down the stairs.

"Can't Matthew just walk downstairs like a normal person?" murmured Molly. She sat up in bed and saw that it was a sunny day. "Yes!" she said. "For the first time all summer, the perfect beach day." She looked over at Amanda, whose eyes were still tightly closed. "And Surf Point Boardwalk, here we come!"

Amanda opened her eyes. "Is Jillian taking us there tonight?" she asked. Jillian was their cousin. She was fourteen and lived near Poppy. Jillian's little brother, John, was about Matthew's age.

"She said she'd take us," replied Molly. "Girls, it's time to get up," called Dad from the bottom of the stairs. "I'm making pancakes."

Amanda and Molly jumped out of bed at the same time. They loved Dad's blueberry pancakes.

After breakfast, there was a mad rush as the Moores quickly packed their bathing suits, towels, and clothes, and attached the kids' bikes to the bike rack on Dad's SUV. They were finally ready for the hour-and-a-half long ride to Surf Point.

"Oops!" cried Matthew, as Dad was pulling out of the parking spot. "I forgot my comic books." No one argued about letting Matthew go back in the house to get them. He was a lot quieter in the car with them.

Poppy was reading the paper on the front porch of his big old white house when they drove up. He waved, and Dad tooted the horn.

"Hi, Poppy!" shouted the twins and Matthew out the car window.

"Hi, Dad," said Mom.

"Hi, everybody!" said Poppy. He was wearing his sun-bleached baseball cap, as usual. He was deeply tanned and his face was creased, but his eyes were bright blue. "I thought you'd never get here! Are you ready for the beach? I packed us a big lunch."

Later, at the beach, after the twins took turns skimming along the shore on a Boogie board, they went under their shady beach umbrella. Matthew and Dad were nearby, showing a little kid how to dig for sand crabs. Mom was hidden under a big hat and dark sunglasses, reading a magazine. Amanda stood behind her chair to read over her shoulder.

"This is the perfect day," Molly told Poppy as she dried off.

Poppy smiled at her. "And what is the perfect day to our Miss Molly Moore?" he asked.

Molly sat down on a towel and hugged her knees. She looked up at Poppy. "The water's not too cold, and we had a picnic, and I found some blue beach glass, and now we're going to get ice-cream sandwiches. But mostly because we're with you!"

Poppy laughed. "That's my girl," he told her.

That night, Aunt Kate, Uncle Jim, Jillian, and John came over to Poppy's for a big fish dinner.

John and Matthew immediately began to wrestle outside in the yard.

Jillian gave both girls a big hug. She smelled like soap and shampoo.

"I like your platform sandals," said Molly.

"Thanks! Mom hates them," replied Jillian. "She thinks they're gonna make me fall flat on my face." Jillian was starting to look really grown-up. She was wearing mascara and purple eyeliner around her brown eyes. Her short brown hair was streaked blond by the summer sun. "I heard you guys are taking a cooking class? That's cool."

"Yeah, it's fun," said Amanda. "Hey, are we going to the boardwalk?"

"Definitely!" said Jillian. "Dad will drop us all off over there after dinner."

Molly, Amanda, and Matthew loved going to the boardwalk, especially at night. They couldn't eat their dinner fast enough.

"*Taste* your food before you swallow it!" cried Poppy.

Finally Uncle Jim was ready to take the kids to the boardwalk. "Now don't eat too much junk food," he ordered as he dropped off the kids at the boardwalk entrance. "I'll pick you up right here in two hours." He looked at Jillian. "Keep everyone together, Jillian," he said. "Don't let anyone wander off."

"I know, Dad!" shouted Jillian over the noise of the carnival music and her cousins slamming the car doors. "Don't worry. Bye!"

The cousins hurried up the wooden-plank stairs to the boardwalk. It was brightly lit and packed with kids, baby strollers, and sunburned grown-ups. The smell of popcorn was everywhere. Loud pop music was blasting out of a pizza parlor.

"What do you want to do first?" asked Jillian. "Play Skee-ball? Whack-A-Mole?"

"Let's get some cotton candy," suggested Amanda.

"Ugh! How can you eat that stuff?" asked Jillian.

"Yeah! Let's eat a whole lot of it—" began John.

"And then we'll ride the roller coaster and it'll make you puke!" cried Matthew. "Ha-ha!" He and John thought they were so funny.

"You just ate, Amanda," said Molly, rolling her eyes. "Give it a rest! Let's play miniature golf."

"Yeah!" shouted Matthew.

"Yeah!" echoed John.

"Okay," said Jillian. "That's way down at the other end, though." She led the way through the crowd, waving at people she knew. It seemed as if she knew everyone.

Something familiar caught Molly's eye. A certain hairstyle, a backpack she'd seen before. She turned back to look.

"Oh my gosh," she cried. "Amanda, *look*!"

Amanda turned around. "What?" she asked.

"Is that who I think it is?" Molly groaned. She pointed to a tall girl with blond hair. "See? Over there, next to the roller coaster?"

"Is that *Natasha*? What is this? Is she *following* us?" Amanda shrieked. Then she remembered something. "You know, I *thought* I saw her today!" she exclaimed. "I thought I was just imagining things. But it *was* her. She was walking with some people on the boardwalk. But she wasn't wearing a bathing suit."

"It's a curse," said Molly. "The Natasha Curse. We're in a different state and we *still* can't get away from her! Uh-oh, she's heading over here." But Molly and Amanda were stuck. The boardwalk was so crowded that the people ahead of them had stopped in their tracks. Once again, there was no avoiding Natasha.

"She hasn't seen us," said Amanda. "Who's she with?"

"I can't tell," replied Molly.

Suddenly the crowd split down the middle and Natasha looked right at the twins. She looked as startled to see them as they'd been to see her. Molly's heart began to pound loudly.

Amanda remembered what Mom had told them about being nice to Natasha. *Here goes nothing*, she thought. *Big smile.*

Meanwhile, Molly was thinking, *how horrible can Natasha be if she's with other people?* She took a deep breath and forced herself to smile. It almost hurt.

"Hi, Natasha," said Molly and Amanda. They held their smiles as long as they could. *We must look so fake*, thought Molly. *Like wax dummies of ourselves.*

"Um—are you having fun?" Molly asked Natasha.

"Hi, Molly, hi, Amanda," said Natasha. She sounded almost scared. "Uh, how are you? It sure is crowded." She looked as if maybe, just maybe, she was smiling. Or trying to.

"We're visiting Poppy—I mean, our grandpa," said Amanda. "He lives near here."

"Oh," said Natasha. "I've never been to Surf Point."

Suddenly, a tall woman with silver hair came over to Natasha. "Come, Natasha," she said, looking at Molly and Amanda. She had the same cold blue eyes as Natasha had. "We're leaving this zoo. It's just too crowded for Daddy and me."

Daddy and me! thought Amanda. *I thought she was Natasha's grandmother.*

What a barrel of fun her mom is, thought Molly.

"But we just got here!" protested Natasha, as her mom pulled her away. "Well, see you later," said Natasha to the twins.

"Okay, see you in class," said Amanda.

Molly and Amanda looked at each other as if to say, *Well, that was weird.* Just then, Matthew shouted, "Come on, you guys! We're waiting for you!"

As Molly and Amanda caught up to Jillian and the boys, Molly said, "We did it! We were nice to Natasha."

"Wait till we tell Mom!" giggled Amanda.

"Mom was right, I *guess,*" commented Molly. "She said if we were nice to Natasha, Natasha just might be nice to us. And I guess she was nice...right?"

"Yeah, she seemed like she was trying to be nice," said Amanda thoughtfully. "But she didn't really get a chance. Her mom seems kind of mean."

"You know, I think I'm actually feeling *sorry* for Natasha!" said Molly with a laugh. "Whoa! What's happening to me?"

"I feel sorry for her, too," replied Amanda. "I mean, she doesn't have any brothers or sisters. And her mom probably doesn't let her do anything. She didn't even let her go swimming today, or stay on the boardwalk tonight for five minutes."

"Her mom *did* let her take the cooking class, though," said Molly.

"That's true," said Amanda.

"Well, anyway—do you think that's why Natasha is mean?" asked Molly. "Because she has a sad life?"

"I don't know," replied Amanda.

The girls fell silent as they walked along. Ahead of them, Jillian, Matthew, and John were laughing together and telling knock-knock jokes.

Over the next two hours, as the cousins putted golf balls, rode the roller coaster, and stuffed their faces with popcorn, Molly and Amanda knew that Natasha couldn't have been having as much fun as they were.

chapter 9

The next morning, as the kids helped Mom pack a picnic lunch for the beach, Mom told them, "Kids, Poppy would like you to stay for a few more days. Dad and I still need to go home today, since we have to work tomorrow."

"But we'll come down after work on Thursday night and pick you up. How does that sound?" asked Dad.

"Woo-hoo!" cheered Matthew.

"Sounds good to me!" exclaimed Molly. "Poppy, can we go crabbing?"

"And can we go back to the boardwalk?" asked Amanda.

"Of course," said Poppy. "And we'll go out for ice cream every night, and stay up as late as we want, and I'll tell you ghost stories!"

And that's exactly what they did for the next few days. Poppy took them for bike rides on the boardwalk. They spent long days swimming and looking for shells with Jillian and John. They watched sharks at the aquarium. They went back to the boardwalk one night, and at the end of the night, finally persuaded Poppy to ride the roller coaster.

"That's the last time I'm ever riding a roller coaster," he told them afterward. "I'm dizzy. Let's go home!"

It seemed as if the Moore kids had been down at the shore forever when Mom and Dad came to pick them up.

"I remember you," joked Dad when he saw the kids.

No one wanted to say good-bye to Poppy, but they knew they'd see him in a few weeks. Soon the Moores were back on the highway heading home. Matthew fell asleep right away, so the car was quiet.

"I almost forgot! We have our cooking class tomorrow," Amanda said, breaking the silence. "I wonder what we'll make this time? I can't wait to see Shawn."

"Me too," Molly whispered. She closed her eyes and slept until they got home.

The next morning, the twins found a note from Mom in the kitchen.

Good morning! I want each of you to practice the piano for an hour this morning, before you go to cooking class. Remember—Mrs. Thatcher is back from vacation next week! I'll be home early today. Have fun in class. Make sure Matthew eats breakfast and takes his vitamin. Love, Mom

"Yipes," said Molly, reading the note. "I forgot our piano teacher is coming home soon. I'm rusty!"

"So am I," said Amanda. "Well, you can go first. I have to make my bed and figure out what I'm going to wear today."

"That'll probably take the whole hour," joked Molly. She looked out the window. Matthew was in the garden, reading a comic book. Molly could tell that he'd eaten breakfast already. There was a trail of crumbs out of the toaster oven, and a half-finished bowl of cereal on the table.

"Matthew," Molly called through the screen door. "Did you take your vitamin?"

"Nope."

"Then get in here and take one." There, she'd done what Mom had asked her to.

After eating some cereal, Molly went straight to the piano. Her fingers felt like spaghetti. Like she'd never played the piano before! *Uh-oh*, she thought. *I hope my fingers aren't like spaghetti in class today. I won't be able to use a knife!*

By the time Molly and Amanda had practiced the piano and made their beds (and Amanda changed her outfit at least three times), the twins were a little late for class. They walked in behind Carmen and quickly slipped into their work stations.

"Hello, everyone!" said Carmen when she walked into class. "It's hot and muggy, so guess what we're going to make today?"

"What?" asked the class.

"Soup!"

"Soup?" exclaimed some of the kids. Soup didn't seem very summery.

"Yes, it's called gazpacho," replied Carmen. "Have you ever heard of it? It's a Spanish dish, and it's delicious in the summer because it's served cold."

"Cold soup?" Lots of the kids laughed.

"Yes! Plus another cold soup made of cucumbers and an herb called dill; poached salmon salad; and for dessert, an apple-and-plum crisp. But the best thing we're going to do is something called *garde-manger*. That is the art of carving fruits and vegetables, making them look pretty. We're going to carve peacocks out of melons! You'll be able to take them home with you."

Peichi spoke up. "Where's Freddie?" she asked.

"Freddie's out of town today, but he'll be back next week," replied Carmen. "Okay, count off. The ones will make the gazpacho, the twos will make the poached salmon salad..."

87

Amanda was with Peichi in the gazpacho group. As the group chopped tomatoes, cucumbers, and peppers, Peichi wouldn't stop talking about her recent day at a new amusement park.

"...so then we went on this ride that dropped you! We were falling and falling like, a million feet down! It was so scary but then I wanted to ride it again! But the line was too long, and my dad said, 'No way, Peichi...'"

"Can somebody turn her off?" muttered Omar. Peichi was so busy talking that she didn't even hear him, or notice David Stern imitating her behind her back.

"Peichi," joked Amanda, "if you keep talking, you're gonna chop up your finger instead of your tomato!"

Later, the class made their honeydew peacocks.

"Mine looks more like a ship," complained Amanda, as the friends left class holding their peacocks.

"At least yours looks like *something*," said Molly. "Mine looks like a blob! Shawn, yours looks the best. It actually looks like a peacock."

Class had seemed so different that day because Freddie hadn't been there to joke with them and help them.

And because Natasha hadn't been there, either.

The twins and Shawn walked to the Moore's house and made some lemonade. They brought it out to the garden, along with a plate of chocolate chip cookies.

 Amanda began to work on a blue beaded bracelet she was making. Molly and Shawn played backgammon. And Kitty pounced on an insect that happened to be in the wrong place at the wrong time.

"Kitty's eating it," exclaimed Shawn. "Gross."

A few minutes later, Shawn looked over at Kitty again. Kitty was now leaning forward, staring very hard at something. It looked like a tiny hand, reaching under the fence.

"Hey!" Shawn whispered to the twins, pointing at the hand. "Look at that!"

Molly and Amanda began to giggle.

"It's Nathan Brewster," whispered Molly. "We've baby-sat him a couple of times. The Brewsters moved in about a month ago. When he hears us talking, he always wants to visit."

"Why doesn't he just shout to us?" Shawn wondered out loud.

"Maybe he thinks he's spying on us," said Molly, laughing.

Amanda jumped up to catch Kitty, who was still

staring at Nathan's hand. Her rear end was wiggling. She was ready to pounce!

"Hi, Nathan," called Molly.

"Hi," answered a little voice on the other side of the fence.

"What are you doing, Nathan?" asked Amanda.

"Who that?"

"It's Amanda. Do you want to come over?"

"Okay."

"I'll be right back," said Amanda, going inside. A minute later, she came back with Nathan, holding his hand. He had coffee-colored skin, dark eyes and hair, and long, dark lashes.

"Hi, Nathan," said Molly and Shawn.

"Hi."

"You're cute, Nathan," said Shawn. "I like your curly hair. And your overalls."

Nathan didn't say anything. He only smiled, showing his tiny white teeth.

"I think Mrs. Brewster was glad to have a break," Amanda told the girls. "She's going to have another baby soon." Amanda looked down at Nathan. "So, Nathan, what's new?"

Nathan held up two fingers.

"You're two?" asked Shawn.

"Cookie?" asked Nathan, looking up at Molly.

90

"*Hmmm*. Well, I don't think your mom will mind if you have just one," said Molly. "Here you go."

"Daddy itchy," announced Nathan. He offered his cookie to Kitty, who ran under the table.

"What, Nathan?"

"Daddy has a rash. On him all over. Itchy bad from mosquito."

"Oh," said Molly. "Um, that's too bad." The girls looked at each other and giggled.

"Little kids say the funniest things!" chuckled Shawn.

Nathan pointed to the fence.

"Do you want to go home? Already?" asked Amanda. Nathan nodded.

"Well, okay, I'll take you. Be right back, guys," said Amanda. "Come on, Nathan, hold my hand."

As Amanda led Nathan out the front door and down the stone steps, she looked down the sloping tree-lined street. Someone was running up the street. It looked like Todd Lewitsky, Matthew's friend. Just then, Amanda heard sirens. A fire truck was on its way somewhere.

"Hi, Todd," called Amanda as Todd approached her.

He looked up at her but didn't stop running. "There's a—house on—fire!" he panted. "I'm going to get my brother."

"What? Whose is it?"

91

"Um, I think it's the McEvoys. They're new." He was passing her now.

Amanda thought for a moment. *The McEvoys? Who are they?* Then it hit her.

"The McElroys!"

Justin McElroy's house was on fire!

chapter 10

Now Amanda thought she could smell smoke. Or was it just her imagination?

"Okay, Nathan, let's skip!" said Amanda. "Or gallop like a horsie!"

The sirens were coming closer.

Nathan wasn't going anywhere. "Fire twuck! Where fire twuck?" he shouted happily. "I wanna see fire twuck!"

"Um, your mommy will take you to see it," said Amanda, clutching Nathan's hand. Inside, she was screaming, *Justin's house is on fire! Justin's house is on fire!*

Just then, Molly and Shawn walked out the front door and looked at Amanda with expressions that said, *what's going on?* Obviously, they'd heard the sirens.

"It's the McElroy's house!" cried Amanda. Then she remembered that she shouldn't scare Nathan. "Come on now, Nathan!" she said, breathing fast. Nathan seemed to suddenly weigh a ton. Even with Amanda pulling him, his feet weren't leaving the ground. So—*ooof!*—she picked him up, which made him scream, "FIRE TWUCK!" She walked quickly over to the Brewsters' and banged on the door.

It took Mrs. Brewster forever to open the door. "Hi, Nate-Nate!" she cooed, propping the door open.

Nathan began to bawl. "*Whaaaaaaaa!*

"Here," said Amanda, handing Nathan to Mrs. Brewster. "There's a fire down the block!"

"What?" asked Mrs. Brewster, but Amanda was already off to catch up with Molly and Shawn, who were running down the street. Other neighbors were opening their doors and looking in the direction of the sirens. Matthew and Ben came running out of Ben's front door and joined the girls.

"I don't see a fire," commented Shawn, as they got closer to the McElroy's house. Everything looked normal, except for the huge fire truck that was coming up Taft Street.

"There's Justin!" cried Amanda. "And Ian!"

Justin and his sixteen year-old brother, Ian, were standing on the sidewalk down from the house. Ian was covering one ear and talking on a cell phone. Justin and Mrs. Tortelli, his next-door neighbor, were watching the fire engine as it came to a stop.

"I hope everybody is okay," Amanda said to her friends.

Four firefighters jumped out of the truck. One talked briefly with Justin and Ian, then went inside.

"Stay back," called a firefighter to the friends.

"I guess we can't go any farther than this," said Shawn to the girls, as the firefighters attached a hose to a fire hydrant.

"That's the engine company," said Matthew, pointing at the truck. "Their truck has the hoses."

"Yeah," added Ben, "and I think the guy that just went in is checking out the fire. Then he'll come out and tell the chief what's going on inside."

How do boys know this stuff? wondered Molly.

More sirens were blaring. In seconds, a police car and three more fire trucks appeared, along with a car that said "Chief."

Molly squinted to see Justin better. "I don't think Justin and his brother look too worried, do you?" she asked Amanda.

"No. I guess their parents are at work. But they must be pretty bummed out," Amanda replied.

"There's the ladder company!" said Matthew, pointing to another truck. "That truck has the ladders and tools and stuff. Wow! Here comes another engine company truck, and—look! There's another engine. This must be a big fire. Aw, man, I wish I could see it!"

"Matthew!" cried Amanda.

"What's the matter with you?" added Molly. "The fire isn't for your—your entertainment!"

"Oh, I didn't mean it that way," said Matthew. "I just

wish I could watch them put the fire *out*. We can't see *anything* from here."

A police officer came up to the little crowd that was forming. "Move back, please," she called out. She had to shout over the noise of the sirens and the firefighters' radios. She placed a barricade between herself and the crowd. The barricade looked like a wooden sawhorse, painted blue. "NYPD," the initials of the New York Police Department, were painted on it in white lettering.

"What's happening?" Matthew asked the police officer.

"A small kitchen fire, but everything's under control," she replied, as she put up the rest of the police barricade.

"Is anybody hurt?" asked Shawn.

"No, everything is under control," replied the police officer as she walked away. Another police officer was heading down the street to block it off to cars.

"The fire's out!" said Ben. "I just heard someone say it over a radio."

More firefighters headed into the house. Some of them had axes.

"What are the axes for?" asked Amanda.

"Oh, that's to open up the walls," replied Ben. "They have to do that."

"Yeah, so that they can check to see if there are fires hidden behind the walls," added Matthew.

"Yipes!" exclaimed Amanda. "So even if the fire is a small one, I guess there's still a lot of damage."

"Look, there's Mrs. McElroy," said Molly, pointing down the street. "Oh, she looks so upset."

The girls watched Mrs. McElroy walk quickly up the street. She was wearing a suit and carrying a briefcase, so she must have come from work. She put her arms around Justin and Ian and pulled them close. It looked as if they were all talking at once, then Mrs. McElroy quickly looked down. She was crying.

"It must be horrible to see a million fire trucks in front of your house," said Amanda sadly. She watched Mrs. Tortelli touch Mrs. McElroy on the shoulder and speak to her. A moment later, Mrs. McElroy and the boys followed Mrs. Tortelli into her house.

The friends stood around for a while with some other neighbors and watched the firefighters' comings and goings. Mrs. Brewster had brought little Nathan. He was excited by all the fire trucks and firefighters.

"I wish we could do something," said Amanda when Mom came home from work. "I feel so bad for the McElroys."

"There is something you can do," said Mom. "I ran

into Peichi and her mom, Song, at the supermarket after work." Mom and Mrs. Cheng knew each other from working at school events together. "They'd heard about the McElroys, too. They figured that the McElroys are going to need a place to stay for a few weeks until they can live in their house again. So Song is going to offer them an apartment in the building they own on Garden Street. It's not far from the McElroy's house, which is perfect, since Justin's parents will have to be there a lot for the contractors." Mom smiled and added, "Song will let them rent it as long as they need it."

"Wow! That's good," said Amanda.

"So," Mom continued, "I think it would really help the McElroys if they didn't have to cook. They probably lost a lot of their kitchen stuff in the fire, and I'm not sure

what the rental will have for them to use. They'll need to buy new things, but they'll have enough on their mind in these next few weeks. Let's spend tomorrow cooking up a lot of food that they can just heat and serve."

"That would be fun!" said Amanda. She pictured a table full of food that she had made: pies, cakes, a turkey with all the trimmings. And Justin would be standing there, amazed that she had done it all just for him and his family.

"We can call Shawn," suggested Molly. "I bet she'd love to help us."

"And Peichi!" added Amanda. "Yeah! Now, what should we make?"

"Casseroles are good," suggested Mom. "And a pasta sauce. And pesto. And pasta salad. And a bean salad. We could even roast a couple of chickens that they can use for sandwiches! And we can bake some cookies and a cobbler.

"This will be so much fun," Mom continued. "I have some vacation days left, so I can take the day off tomorrow." She put her arms around her daughters and pulled them in for a hug. "Cooking with my girls!"

To: qtpie490
From: mooretimes2
mooretimes2: wuzzup, Shawn? Give us the dish!
qtpie490: hi. What do u mean, the dish?
mooretimes2: "the dish" means "what's new?" So, what's the dish?
qtpie490: nothing to "dish" about! Bored 2nite. Wuzzup with you?
mooretimes2: we're on a mission! We need u! Peichi too.
qtpie490: name the mission, Agents Moore
mooretimes2: Mission McElroy!
qtpie490: name the purpose of Mission McElroy
mooretimes2: feed cute Justin and his family. Ya cookin' with us?
qtpie490: :-@   :-@   :-@
mooretimes2: we'd knew you'd scream! We are the fabulous Chef Girls!
qtpie490: GMTA. What will we make?
mooretimes2: everything!
qtpie490: LOL

mooretimes2: Mom's gonna help big time

qtpie490: whew!

mooretimes2: what's Peichi's sn?

qtpie490: don't know, sry

mooretimes2: sry?

qtpie490: sorry

mooretimes2: oh, duh! G2G. Come by 2morrow, and cook!!!

qtpie490: b-b

mooretimes2: L8R! mwa***

qtpie490: <3   <3   <3   <3   <3
(hearts, get it? My cousin showed me.)

"I just had a weird idea," Molly told Amanda that night, after they'd instant-messaged Shawn, and were brushing their teeth.

Amanda looked up into the mirror. "What's that?" she asked, the toothbrush still in her mouth.

"We could invite Natasha over to cook with us."

Amanda's mouth dropped open. Blue toothpaste gushed out of her mouth and down her chin.

"Whoops!" she said. The twins began to laugh so hard that they had to spit out all their toothpaste.

"That's big, Molly!" exclaimed Amanda. "To actually invite Natasha over here?"

"Well," said Molly, "what do you think?"

"She'd never come. She wasn't even in class the other day."

Molly shrugged. "Let's call her tomorrow and find out."

The next morning, Molly and Amanda called Peichi.

"Hi, Peichi! It's Molly and Amanda. Did we wake you up?"

"Oh! Hi!" exclaimed Peichi. She sounded surprised to hear from the twins. Even though she'd known them forever, they didn't call each other or hang out too often. "I've been up for a while," said Peichi. "I've already practiced my flute!"

"What are you doing today?" Amanda asked her.

"Not much," replied Peichi. "We're building a pool in our backyard and it's almost ready, but I still can't go swimming in it yet! Maybe tomorrow, though! So I really don't have anything to do today! How boring!"

"You're going to have a *pool*? That's so cool," said Amanda.

"A cool pool!" joked Molly.

"Yeah!" said Peichi. "I can't wait! Anyway, what are you doing?"

"Operation Feed the McElroys!" replied the twins.

"Wow! What's that?" asked Peichi.

"We're going to cook all day until we fall over," replied Molly.

"For the McElroys," added Amanda. "We heard that your mom and dad helped them with the apartment."

"Yeah!" said Peichi. "They have one that's empty right now."

"Anyway," continued Amanda, "We wanted to do something, too. Mom's helping us. She took the day off. Do you want to come over and cook with us?"

"Oh!" said Peichi, "that's *great! I'd* like to help Justin's family, too! Okay! I'll be over. What time? Do you want me to bring anything? What are we going to make?"

Molly and Amanda looked at each other and giggled. Peichi was so funny.

"We'll call you when we get back from the store," replied Amanda. "Okay? Oh, but there's one other little thing."

"What?" asked Peichi.

"Well," began Amanda.

"Natasha Ross might come over, too," blurted Molly.

"Natasha Ross!"

"Yeah, it's a long story," said Amanda with a giggle. "We haven't called her yet. She probably won't come anyway."

"Whatever!" said Peichi. "I don't care. She doesn't bother *me.*"

"Okay, good," said Molly and Amanda. "We'll call you when we get home. Bye!"

"Okay, *great!*" said Peichi. "Bye!"

Molly hung up the phone. "Well," she said. "Should we call Natasha now?"

Amanda hesitated. "Maybe we should wait until we get back from the store," she suggested.

"Why?"

"I don't know...because I want to put off calling her as long as possible, that's why!" replied Amanda with a giggle.

"It's now or never," said Molly firmly. "Do or die." She looked up the number in the Park Terrace phone book. "Let's see, R-O-S-S. There are lots of Rosses, but I know she lives on Garden Street...she and Justin will be neighbors. Here goes!" she said, dialing the number.

Natasha's mother answered the phone.

"Hello, is Natasha there?" asked Molly.

There was a pause. "Who's calling, please?"

Molly cleared her throat. "This is Amelia Moore," she answered. Amanda shot her a look that said, *Why did you say Amelia?*

There was another pause. "Just a moment."

It took a while for Natasha to answer the phone. "Hello?" She sounded weirded out.

"Hi, Natasha, it's Molly and Amanda." Molly was hoping she sounded nice, nice, nice.

"Oh, hi! Uh, how are you guys? Er—did you have fun at the boardwalk?"

"Oh, yeah, it was fun. So was class this week."

Natasha didn't say anything.

"Um," Molly went on, "do you know Justin McElroy?"

"No."

"Oh, he's this new kid on our block. He's in our grade. Anyway, they had a small fire, and they can't live in their house until they fix up the kitchen and get rid of the smoky smell, and he's actually going to be living on your street for a few weeks until the kitchen is fixed...we're going to cook some food for them today. Do you want to come over?"

"Um, let me check," replied Natasha.

The twins heard muffled voices. Natasha had put her hand over the speaker. She must have been talking with her mom.

"Hello?" said Natasha. "No, I can't. But—um, thanks for asking me. Bye."

Click.

She'd hung up.

Molly looked at the phone receiver. "Buh-bye," she said to it. "Well, that was weird."

"I told you she wouldn't come," said Amanda. "But—we tried!"

"Ready, girls?" Mom called up from the kitchen.

Molly and Amanda ran downstairs. They hopped into Mom's old car and headed to the store.

Choice Foods was empty because it was early in the morning.

"I love coming here in the morning," said Mom. She and the twins got everything they needed in no time. Two whole chickens. A cantaloupe. Bananas. Pork chops. Sliced cheese for sandwiches. Fresh basil. Romaine lettuce. Penne pasta. Two loaves of bread. Blueberries. Nectarines. Canned plum tomatoes. Mustard, mayonnaise, butter, since the McElroys needed everything. Salt. Pepper. And a lot more.

"Whew!" said Amanda as she lugged in a heavy bag of groceries from the car.

"We practically bought out the store," said Molly.

"What should we do first?" asked Amanda, eyeing all the grocery bags on the kitchen floor.

"First," said Mom, "we have to prepare everything. Molly, please get the salad spinner to rinse the basil. Amanda, you can put the blueberries in the colander and rinse them off. I'll rinse the nectarines and cut them up."

"I'll give Peichi and Shawn a call to let them know we're home," said Molly.

By the time Peichi and Shawn got to the Moores' house, the twins and Mom were on a roll. They'd almost finished making their first dish.

"That looks good," Shawn said.

"What is it, Mrs. Moore?" asked Peichi.

"Blueberry-and-nectarine cobbler," said Mom. "It's my favorite summer dessert."

"Mine, too, Mom," Amanda reminded her.

"*Everything's* your favorite summer dessert!" Molly teased Amanda.

"The uncooked fruit is on the bottom," Mom told Peichi and Shawn. "For the top, I just make an easy sugar cookie batter that I spoon on. Now I'll chill it, and the McElroys can bake it. It'll have a nice crust when it comes out of the oven."

By lunchtime, Mom had helped the girls make pesto, an easy pasta sauce out of fresh basil, olive oil, and pine nuts. And they'd used Carmen's recipe, the one they made in class, for the pasta sauce made from plum tomatoes.

They took a break and ate sandwiches and lemonade in the garden while Kitty dozed in the shade.

"Where's Matthew?" asked Amanda.

"At Ben's, of course," said Mom with a laugh. "He's

eating dinner over there. I think that the four of us will go out for dinner."

Suddenly Molly sat straight up and said "Hey!"

"Hey *what?*" asked Amanda.

"I just had an idea," replied Molly. "We are the Chef Girls, and the Chef Girls need to write a cookbook that they can give to all their friends and fans!"

"What would be in the cookbook?" Peichi wanted to know.

"Everything we've ever made!" replied Molly.

Amanda nudged Shawn. "You're the artist, Shawn," she said. "You've got really pretty handwriting, too. You could write the recipes! I have a big blank book upstairs that we can use."

"Actually," said Shawn, "we could *all* write the recipes. And we could all draw little pictures and put glitter on the pages, too."

Molly cried, "We can call it 'The Dish!'"

"Or just 'Dish,'" suggested Amanda. "It sounds a little cooler."

"Yeah!" cried all the girls.

"That's a great idea!" said Mom. "Well, Chef Girls, it's time to get back into the kitchen."

So everyone went back to work. It was really Mom who did most of the work, but the girls were a big help. They learned a lot about cooking just by helping her.

They roasted the chickens. They made a homemade barbecue sauce to go with the pork chops. They made homemade Caesar salad dressing for the romaine lettuce.

"It's gonna be so fun to show up and surprise Justin with all this food," said Shawn.

"What is Justin like?" asked Peichi. "I don't know him."

"Ask Amanda," giggled Molly. "Or Shawn. They think he's supercute!"

"He's nice," said Amanda, turning red.

"Sure, he's nice," said Molly with a shrug. "But I don't see what's so great about him. He's just another boy."

"Yeah, what's so great about boys anyway?" asked Peichi. "I think they're—obnoxious! They're loud! They burp! They throw food in the cafeteria! I mean, I guess some of them are okay to be friends with, but I don't want them to be my *boyfriend* or anything like that."

"Well, anyway, I can't wait to see Justin's face when he sees all this," said Amanda.

"Yeah!" Peichi said. "His eyeballs are going to pop out of his head!" Everyone laughed.

"And we're not even finished yet!" exclaimed Mom. "Now we'll make a bean salad. That's good in the summer. Oh! We can make a pasta salad, too. And then I think we're finished!" She smiled. "Unless you want to whip up some brownies."

"Okay!" said all the girls.

"But let's make a double batch,"
suggested Amanda "One pan
will be just for us!"

chapter 12

Finally, all the food was ready.

"Peichi, did your mom write down Mrs. McElroy's cell phone number for me?" asked Mom.

"Here it is," said Peichi, pulling a piece of paper out of her pocket.

"Thanks," said Mom, reading the note. "Brenda McElroy. Okay..."

Mom began to dial the phone, and told the girls, "She should be there now. I'll give her a call to make sure someone is there to answer the door." The girls all looked at each other and began to giggle nervously. It was almost time to deliver the food to Justin!

"Hello, is this Brenda McElroy?" asked Mom. "Hi, I'm your neighbor Barbara Moore...I was so sorry to hear about the fire! And I'm glad no one was hurt... You'll be back in your house in about three weeks? Oh, that's great! Well, my daughters and some of their friends and I have made up some food to help you through this week! Oh, it was no trouble. We had fun doing it! My girls know Justin—oh, you met them at the store, that's right...yes, they do like to cook!

Okay, we'll bring it over. See you in about ten minutes. Bye!"

Mom helped the girls put all the food in sturdy plastic containers and on some colorful ceramic platters that she covered with plastic wrap.

"I've never seen these dishes before, Mom," said Amanda.

"I haven't used them since before you were born," commented Mom, as she began to carefully place the containers in a box. "I've been waiting to sell them in a garage sale. But I'm glad I haven't gotten around to it, because now the McElroys can have them. I have some old silverware, too, that I used in college! I'll bet they can use it."

Mom went down to the basement to get some boxes and the old silverware. She came up with pink paper napkins too.

"Those napkins say, 'Happy Birthday,'" Amanda said.

"Oh, Amanda, it doesn't *matter*," retorted Molly.

"Mrs. Moore, maybe we could cut some flowers and bring them in a vase," suggested Shawn. "To decorate their table."

"That's a great idea," replied Mom. "Why don't you go into the garden and cut some of my roses and bring them in? I know

I have an old vase around here somewhere. It's ugly, but we could put a bow on it and no one will notice!"

"A *bow?*" said Molly, wrinkling her nose. "Well, okay."

"Maybe we shouldn't bring the roses," said Amanda suddenly.

"Why?" asked everyone else, including Mom.

"Because maybe Justin will think—he'll think that we're—I'm—we're—being, uh, too fussy," said Amanda. "Like, *romantic.*"

Everyone began to laugh. Amanda laughed too, but her face was red.

"Don't worry, sweetie," Mom told her. "It's just the centerpiece for the table! No one will think anything of it! And flowers make such a difference. Think how you would feel if suddenly you were living in a strange new place." Mom put her hand on Amanda's shoulder. "Remember, Manda, we're doing this for all the McElroys, not only Justin!"

"Okay," said Amanda. She smiled at Shawn. "It is a good idea, Shawn."

Amanda went with Shawn to cut the best roses while Mom searched for the old vase.

Everyone laughed when Mom came down from the attic with the vase. It *was* ugly, with its dull beige color and odd shape.

"It looks like an onion," Shawn pointed out. She

began to arrange the roses, then stepped back. "This is hard!" she said. "What a mess. Mrs. Moore, can you make it look better?"

In just a few seconds, Mom made the bouquet look pretty. She cut some of the stems so that all of the roses weren't the same height. "There!" she said. "And now for the finishing touch!" She wrapped a red velvet bow, left over from a Christmas gift, around the vase. "Time to go!" she announced.

"Just a minute," said Amanda. She ran upstairs.

"Uh-oh, Amanda's going to change her outfit," said Molly, rolling her eyes. She sighed and sat down at the kitchen table as if to say, *This is going to take a while!*

"Hurry, Amanda," called Mom from the bottom of the stairs.

"She's probably looking for an evening gown," snickered Molly, as Mom walked back into the kitchen. Shawn and Peichi laughed.

Mom playfully tousled Molly's hair. "Meanwhile, I practically have to beg you to brush your hair once in a while," she chuckled. "So don't make fun of your sister."

Amanda rushed downstairs. She was wearing her new dark blue denim capris with white stitching around the pockets, a new white top, and sparkly beaded navy blue flip-flops. "I'm ready now," she announced.

"Very nice," said Mom.

"I love your flip-flops!" Peichi told Amanda. "They're great! I want a pair of those!"

"Okay, let's go!" said Shawn.

The girls picked up the boxes and carried them to the street, where Mom's car was parked. Amanda made a face. Mom's car was so embarrassing. It was a big old Cadillac. Its body was painted a weird color that was trying to look gold. The top was black. Why couldn't Mom have a white SUV like all the other moms? But Mom loved her big old gold car. She'd inherited it from her favorite aunt, Aunt Hazel. *I hope we park far away from Justin's apartment*, thought Amanda. She wondered why the car didn't ever seem to embarrass Molly.

After putting the boxes in the roomy trunk, everyone got in the car. Shawn held the vase on her lap in the front seat.

"This car is great!" said Peichi.

"Really?" asked Amanda.

"Yeah! It's so big! It's like a boat!"

It only took a few minutes to drive to 242 Garden Street. "This is it," said Peichi.

"Oh, good," said Mom. "There's a parking space right in front!" Amanda rolled her eyes. *Yeah, that's just great, Mom*, she thought.

The girls looked up at the pretty brick row house

with flower boxes in all the windows. Peichi told them that the McElroys' apartment was on the top floor. Everyone got out of the car and took a box out of the trunk.

"You go first, Mom," said Amanda. So Mom led the way up the three steps that led to the main door. She buzzed the top apartment.

"Who is it?" crackled a boy's voice through a speaker. Was it Justin? The girls giggled.

"Hello, it's Barbara Moore," said Mom. "And company."

"Okay," said the voice. There was a loud buzzing sound that made Amanda jump, and the door unlocked automatically. Everyone came in the entry and began to walk up the two flights of stairs. Their footsteps echoed. They could hear a door creak open on the top floor.

"Hello!" called Mom in her "cheerful" voice.

"Hello!" answered Mrs. McElroy. "Come on up!"

Stomp, stomp, went everyone's feet up the stairs. Mrs. McElroy was waiting for them with the door open. "Hi, everybody!" she said. "Wow! Look at all the boxes! And roses, too!" She smiled at Mom and said, "Hi, Barbara, I'm Brenda."

"It's so nice to meet you, Brenda," said Mom.

"Come on in, everybody!" said Mrs. McElroy. "Oh, I just can't believe what you've done!" She ushered everyone in the door. "Hello, girls, it's nice to see you again," she said warmly to the twins as they passed her.

"Hi! I'm Amanda." She gave Mrs. McElroy an extra-big smile, then she looked beyond the door for Justin.

"Hi, I'm Molly."

"Hel-*lo*! I'm Peichi Cheng!"

"Oh, you're Song's daughter!" said Mrs. McElroy. "We're so grateful to your mom and dad."

"Hi, Mrs. McElroy, I'm Shawn Jordan. It's nice to meet you."

"Hi, Shawn, it's so nice to meet you," said Mrs. McElroy. She gestured to Justin and Ian, who were standing at the entry to the kitchen. "Here are my boys. This is Justin, and that's Ian!"

Justin and Ian waved awkwardly. "Hi," they both said, as they began to take the boxes from the girls.

"Wow! This is a lot of food!" said Ian, looking inside the boxes. He looked up at the girls with a grin. "This is really great. Thank you." Then he quickly shot Justin a stern look that meant, *Say something polite, you bonehead!*

"Thanks a lot," said Justin. He was blushing. *So Justin's shy*, thought Amanda. *That's so cute.* "Um, we were just waiting for Dad to come home," Justin added. "Then we were going to go out for dinner. But this looks a lot better!"

"Wow! Two roasted chickens! Tomato sauce! And look at this," exclaimed Ian, as he held up a glass baking pan. "What's the stuff on top?"

"That's a cobbler," Amanda spoke up. "You need to bake it. The stuff on top is the crust. I like it a lot!"

"You're not getting any of this, Ian!" Justin told Ian. He took the pan from Ian and looked at it. "This is all mine!" Now Justin didn't seem so shy anymore.

"You'll share it with all of us, buddy," chuckled Mrs. McElroy. She looked at Mom and said, "But I know he could eat the whole thing by himself!"

"That's right," said Mom. "So—what exactly happened with the fire? Was it a bad fire?"

"Justin and I were in the kitchen," replied Ian. "I smelled smoke, and then we saw smoke coming from one of the outlets—"

"Then there was this sound, like, POP!" interrupted Justin.

"And then a small flame," Ian went on. "We called 911 right away."

"It turned out that the wiring in the kitchen was very old and in bad shape," added Mrs. McElroy. She sighed. "It seems like we just moved in, and then we had to move out again! But my husband, Scott, and I are just glad the boys weren't hurt. They were home at the time. I was on my way home from the office, and Scott was on a business trip." She smiled at Peichi. "The Chengs have been wonderful," she added. "Song called us only an hour after the firefighters left. We knew right away that we had a place to go."

"Was there much damage?" asked Mom.

"Not really," replied Ian.

"Until the firefighters got there," added Mrs. McElroy. "There's some minor water damage from the hoses, of course. And the firefighters had to open up the walls and the ceiling to make sure there were no other fires. So they'll have to be repaired."

"It *was* kind of cool when the firefighters brought in the water vacs to suck up the water," said Justin.

That made Mrs. McElroy roll her eyes. "Boys," she said jokingly. "Well, thank you again—so much! I know we'll all enjoy this delicious food."

"Yes, thank you very much," echoed Justin and Ian.

"You're welcome!" said the girls all at the same time. That made everybody laugh.

Then Mrs. McElroy's eyes welled up with tears. She looked away for a moment, then turned back to Mom and the girls. "We're a long way from Chicago, where we came from," she said. "It's so nice to know that we've moved to a community where people really care about each other."

"We like Brooklyn," stated Ian. "It's like living in a small town, even though it's so close to Manhattan."

Justin nodded. "I like it better than living in the suburbs," he added.

"Well, we had fun doing the cooking," said Amanda, looking at Justin.

"Yeah! And we did it all today!" said Peichi. "We just kept cooking and cooking!" Everyone laughed again.

"Please keep the dishes and silverware," Mom told Mrs. McElroy. "They're old. You'd be doing me a favor!"

Mrs. McElroy laughed as she showed everyone to the door. "All right," she replied. "Thanks again for everything!"

"Bye," said Justin and Ian.

Amanda couldn't help turning around to see Justin on her way out the door. He waved at her. She waved and turned back around quickly so that he couldn't see that her face was turning red.

"'Bye!" said Mom and the girls. They headed back down the stairs and got back in the car.

"We did it!" exclaimed Molly. "Operation Feed the McElroys!" Everyone gave each other high-fives.

"Did you see how happy they looked?" said Peichi.

"They sure were surprised," added Amanda. "I've never really helped anyone like that before."

"It feels good to do something nice for someone else. And it was fun because they weren't even expecting it," said Shawn. "That was the best part!"

Mom started the car. "Right!" she said. "They thought they were all on their own. I'm glad I took the day off to do that. It does feel good to help. And I'm proud of all of you girls for wanting to help."

Mom backed the car out of the tight parking spot. "Okay, Shawn and Peichi, I'll drive you home now."

As Mom headed down Garden Street, Molly gasped. "Look who it is!" she said. "On the sidewalk over there!"

"Natasha," said Amanda. "Mom, why are you slowing *down*?"

"So you can say hi to her, silly."

"Maybe she won't want to talk to all of us," said Amanda. Mom stopped the car anyway, but Natasha, who was walking a small dog, was involved in her own thoughts. She didn't hear the car.

Shawn and Peichi lowered their windows. "Hi, Natasha!" called Peichi loudly. "Over here!" That made everyone giggle, even Mom.

Natasha was startled. She turned around, then when she realized who it was, began to slowly walk toward the car, her little terrier following on its leash.

Natasha bent down to see everyone in the car. "Hi," she said. She smiled, but it was a brief, sad smile.

"Hi, Natasha," said Molly.

"Hello," said Mrs. Moore to Natasha. "It's nice to meet you, Natasha."

"Hello, Mrs. Moore."

"We just delivered all the food to Justin's family," Amanda told Natasha. "We cooked all day today."

"Really? That sounds like fun," said Natasha. "I wish—"

Just then, everyone heard a woman's voice call severely, "Natasha! Who are you talking to?" It was Mrs. Ross, standing on the steps of their house, a few doors up the street.

Natasha stood up, and the girls couldn't see her face anymore.

"Just some friends, Mom," she said.

"Who?"

"Just some *friends*," Natasha said, louder this time.

"It's time to come in," said her mother.

Natasha bent down again and looked in the car. "I have to go," she said. "It was nice to meet you, Mrs. Moore."

"Bye," said everyone, but Natasha had already turned away and was hurrying toward home.

Everyone was quiet as Mom began to drive again.

"Poor Natasha," said Mom. "She seems so sad."

Molly was beginning to have an idea about Natasha. "Mom, do you think that maybe Natasha *wanted* to cook with us today?" asked Molly. "And her mom just didn't let her?"

"Yeah," added Amanda. "Maybe she doesn't really hate us after all."

"That could be the case," replied Mom. "Maybe her mother is overprotective and doesn't let her do much outside of the house. When I was about your age, I had a friend who wasn't allowed to do much of anything."

"Oh," said Molly. She looked out the window and tried to picture what it would be like if Mom never let her and Amanda and Matthew do anything. Well, at least they could still play with each other. But Natasha didn't have any brothers or sisters.

"I hope that you'll keep inviting her to do things," said Mom. "Maybe her mom will come around after a while. I think Natasha needs to have some fun! Does she have many friends?"

The girls thought for a moment. "She had one friend," Shawn said. "Remember Monica what's-her-name?"

"Monica Aguilar," said Peichi. "She moved to Washington, D.C., last year. So Natasha's been pretty lonely for a while, I'll bet."

"Why do you think Natasha lied and said those terrible things about Molly and Amanda and me last year? She sure acted like she hated us then," Shawn asked Mrs. Moore.

"People sometimes lash out when they're unhappy," Mrs. Moore replied. "That's how they deal with their angry feelings. They try to make other people feel as bad as they do...well, here we are." She stopped at Shawn's house. "Shawn, tell your dad I said hello."

"Thanks, Mrs. Moore," said Shawn, as she got out of the car. "I'll see you guys tomorrow. This was fun. Bye!"

"Bye!" called the girls.

"Next stop, Peichi's house," announced Mom. "Then we'll pick up Dad and go to Luigi's restaurant. Let someone else do the cooking!"

To: mooretimes2
From: happyface
happyface: hi mooretimes2!

mooretimes2: wuzzup peichi? What's the dish? LOL

happyface: I had fun being a Chef Girl today! Thank u for asking me.

mooretimes2: We couldn't have done Mission McElroy without u!!!!

happyface: what did u have for dinner at Luigi's?

mooretimes2: major spaghetti and manicotti! Stuffed our faces!

happyface: sounds really great! Hey do u want 2 come over to my house tomorrow? They are finished building the pool in our back yard! And there is water in it!!!!!!!

mooretimes2: we are there! ☺ ☺

happyface: OK! I'll call Shawn.

mooretimes2: sry, GTG, mom sez go 2 bed.

happyface: me 2. I'm glad we are getting to be better friends. See you 2morrow! Here's a rose for you.   @>>-->>---

mooretimes2: cool! b-b

Molly and Amanda hadn't been at Peichi's house since Peichi's eighth birthday party. The house was huge, and old, and had stained-glass windows on the front door.

"A friend with a pool!" said Molly, after she rang Peichi's bell. "Our summer is getting better and better!"

"Hi-eeee!" said Peichi, opening the front door. She was wearing blue boy shorts with giant flowers on them, and a matching bikini top. Her hair was in one long braid down her back. "Come on in! Shawn just got here! I can't wait to show you the pool!"

Peichi led the twins downstairs through the game room and out a sliding glass door. The girls stepped out onto a pretty wooden deck. The oval pool seemed huge. Near the pool was a small table with an umbrella and four chairs.

Shawn, wearing a white one-piece suit, was already swimming. "Hi!" she called.

"Hi, Shawn! Wow, this is nice, Peichi!" said Molly. "I forgot how big your backyard is!"

"It's so pretty," said Amanda.

"It's not even finished yet," said Peichi. "Mom's putting flowers in. She says it'll look even better in a few weeks. You should see the pool at night! We turned the lights on last night, and it like glowed! I can't wait to have a pool party sleepover! My mom's at the store, she'll be back in a minute. Do you want something to drink? We have juice, Coke, orange soda..." Peichi stopped to take a breath.

"Juice is fine," said Amanda. "Molly wants orange

soda, right, Molls?" Molly had already taken off the shorts she'd put on over her green glitter-fabric tankini, and was heading into the pool.

"Sounds good, whatever!" said Molly as she jumped in.

"I'm going to be your waitress!" giggled Peichi. "I'll be right back!"

Amanda peeled off her shorts and T-shirt. Like Peichi, she was wearing boy shorts and a matching top. It was pale yellow with gold-and-green sparkles.

"Watch out! Here I come!" shouted Amanda, jumping in the pool.

Just then, Mrs. Cheng opened the sliding glass door. "Hello, girls," she said. "It's nice to see you again. It sounds like you had an adventure yesterday."

"Hello, Mrs. Cheng!" cried all the girls.

Mrs. Cheng looked like a model. She had big black sunglasses on, wide-leg jeans with a drawstring waist, a red-and-white striped T-shirt, and high cork wedgie sandals. Her shiny black hair was chin-length and parted in the middle.

"I need to go back to work now," said Mrs. Cheng. "But I've set out some mini-pizzas for you. Peichi can put them in the toaster oven if you get hungry. There are baby carrots, too. See you later!"

"What is your mom's job, Peichi?" asked Shawn when

Peichi came out with the drinks and potato chips. She set them on the table, and everyone got out of the water for a snack.

"Mom's a graphic designer," replied Peichi. "She has an office upstairs. Like, if someone is making a poster or a ketchup label or whatever, she decides what kind of lettering to use, and what little pictures to put on it. Stuff like that. She paints pictures, too. Mom's a really good artist!"

"That sounds neat," said Shawn. "Maybe that's what I'll do when I grow up."

"I think I want to help people when I grow up," said Molly.

"Me too!" cried Peichi.

"Doing what?" asked Amanda, looking at her sister.

"I don't know," said Molly. "But yesterday was so fun, helping the McElroys."

"I thought it was exciting," said Shawn. "It was like we were working in a restaurant. We were doing a million things at once!"

"The McElroys were so happy and surprised," added Peichi. "It was so fun to watch their faces when they saw all the food!"

"We were a good team yesterday," said Amanda, taking a handful of potato chips.

"Well, we are the fabulous Chef Girls!" exclaimed Shawn.

"It would be fun to do that again," Molly told the girls. "I wish we could...maybe there's someone else we could cook for."

"I know!" said Amanda. "We've started writing a cookbook. So why don't we start our own club? A cooking club?"

"You mean, like meet once a week to get together and cook?" asked Peichi.

"Uh-huh, after our cooking class ends in a few weeks. Or maybe even start right away."

"That sounds like fun," said Shawn. "And that way, we'll keep writing down recipes for 'Dish.'"

"And my mom can help us with the design!" added Peichi. "She'd make the cover look really cool."

"Who would we be cooking for?" asked Shawn. "I mean, who would eat the food?"

"Our families would, since our parents are so busy," replied Molly. "I don't know about you guys, but Amanda and I get pretty sick of take-out dinners all the time! That's why we started cooking in the first place!"

Shawn and Peichi laughed. They knew what the twins were talking about.

"Maybe we could take turns—you know, cook for one of our families, then another," suggested Shawn.

"And if there is someone to help, then we'd cook for them instead," added Peichi.

"But you know, we never could have done all that cooking for Justin, um, I mean the McElroys, without Mom," Amanda reminded Molly. Her face was turning red because everyone laughed when she said "Justin."

"Oh, that's true," said Molly. "Hmmm. Well, we will get to be better and better cooks as we take our classes. And our parents won't be so worried that we're going to cut off our fingertips or burn down the house if they're not around."

"What day should we meet?" asked Shawn.

"How about Sunday?" suggested Peichi. "That way, if we do need one of our parents to help us, they'll always be around."

"Right," said Molly. "Our mom loves to be in the kitchen on the weekends anyway."

"And my dad does, too!" said Peichi.

"We could have special guest chefs!" said Molly. "Like, Peichi, your dad could show us how to cook Chinese food!"

"And my Grandma Ruthie could show us how to cook Southern food!" added Shawn. "When she comes to visit next time."

"Maybe we could even set up a video camera and film our own cooking shows!"

"My dad has a tripod we could use!"

"This is gonna be so *great*!"

chapter **124**

olly and Amanda left Peichi's house late in the afternoon. Mom would be home soon. For now, the twins had the garden to themselves.

"These poor roses need water," said Molly. She turned on the hose.

"Hi!" called Nathan over the fence. "Hi! I'm Nathan!"

"Hi, Nathan," said the twins.

"Mommy has a tummy ache," he called.

"Daddy has itchy mosquito bites, Mommy's tummy hurts, what next?" joked Molly.

Amanda jumped out of her chair. "Because she's going to have her *baby*, that's why!"

"Oh! Right! Yipes!" said Molly. "Um, should we go over there?"

"Yeah!" said Amanda. "Maybe she needs help or something!"

"I hope not," muttered Molly as they walked quickly through the kitchen and out the front door.

Amanda ran up to the Brewster's door and rang the doorbell.

"Maybe we should just open the door?" Molly suggested.

131

"Okay." Amanda pushed the door open. "Hello, Mrs. Brewster? It's Molly and Amanda."

Mrs. Brewster waddled into view. "Oh, hi, girls," she said. She looked surprised and a little confused.

"Sorry," said the twins. They did "the twin thing" and turned beet red at the same time.

"We were, uh, worried—" began Amanda.

"Because Nathan is calling over the fence that you have a tummy ache!" interrupted Molly. "We thought you were having your baby right now by yourself!"

"Really?" said Mrs. Brewster. She chuckled and walked slowly toward the twins. "My smart little Nathan. Well, he's right, I am going to have my baby! I just called my husband, and we're off to the hospital soon. It's a little sooner than we expected, and I was just trying to reach a baby-sitter."

"Oh, we can watch Nathan!" said Molly. "He can stay at our house and have dinner with us."

"Right," added Amanda. "He can sleep over, too. It's not a problem at all."

Mrs. Brewster's face relaxed. "Oh," she said, "thank you so much. One less thing for me to deal with right now! Sam and I will bring him over when we're ready to leave."

"Okay," said the twins. They turned and walked outside.

"See you soon!" said Mrs. Brewster.

"Yipes," said Molly as they walked back into the house. "It must be so weird to know you're going to have a baby!"

"I'm just glad she isn't having it right now," said Amanda. "We'd have to, like, call 911 and be those hero kids you're always seeing on the news."

"I'm not ready to help deliver babies," said Molly with a laugh. "Let's stick to cooking to help people! Looks like it's time for Operation Feed the Brewsters!"

"Nathan, do you like potatoes?" asked Molly. The family was seated at the table in the garden, waiting for Dad to finish grilling the chicken.

"Where's my mommy and daddy?" asked Nathan sadly. He'd been at the Moore's for an hour, and was ready to go home.

"Your mommy is having her baby, remember?" said Amanda.

"Yeah, Nathan! Just think, soon you'll have a baby brother or a baby sister!" Matthew told him.

Nathan began to cry. "Don't want one," he sniffled. "Want Mommy. I'm hungry."

"Good!" said Mom, carrying out a bowl of crisp

roasted potatoes and a green salad. "Because dinner's ready, and we're going to feed you until you're a roly-poly!" That made Nathan giggle. Soon he was so busy eating that he forgot to miss his mommy.

"So guess what?" said Molly to Mom and Dad when Dad brought over the platter of chicken.

"I give up!" said Dad. He always said that. It was his little joke left over from when the twins and Matthew were little and used to say, "Guess what?" all the time.

"The Chef Girls are going to have a cooking club," announced Amanda. "With Shawn and Peichi. Every Sunday, we'll get together to cook!"

"Who's gonna eat the rat poison, I mean food?" asked Matthew.

"You will!" said Molly. "We'll make you be the guinea pig."

"Anyway, before we were so *rudely* interrupted," continued Amanda, "tomorrow we'll make something for Nathan and Mr. Brewster." Nathan looked up when he heard his name. He smiled at Amanda and held out a piece of potato for her.

"That's a nice idea," said Mom. "But remember, I won't be here to help you. I can't take another day off so soon."

"That's okay, Mom," Molly assured her. "We're going to make some pesto, that's easy. We'll throw in a box of pasta for Mr. Brewster to cook. We can make a salad. And that cobbler was no big deal to make. It'll be easy!"

"Hold it!" said Dad with a laugh. "Did you all decide together on what you'd make?"

The twins looked at each other. "No," they said.

"You're not the kings of the club," said Matthew. "Or, you know, the *queens.*"

"Save it, Matthew," said Dad.

"You'll need to buy groceries each week," Mom reminded the girls. "How will you pay for them?"

"Um, right," said Amanda. "We didn't talk about that yet either, but between the four of us, we can pay for it out of our allowance. If some of us don't have money, we just can't cook, that's all. But we could still meet to work on our cookbook."

"You could pay dues each week," said Dad. "And that would go toward your food."

"That's a good idea, Dad," Molly said.

"And with a pool of money, we'll always know how much we have to spend!" Amanda added.

Mr. Brewster called the Moores late that night to report that Mrs. Brewster was fine. She'd had a beautiful baby girl, named Charlotte.

"Congratulations! That's wonderful!" Mrs. Moore told

135

him. "Nathan missed you, but he did so well tonight. He's been asleep a long time. He'll be glad to see you tomorrow."

Early the next morning while Mom and Dad were getting ready for work, Mr. Brewster came by to pick up Nathan.

"When is Mrs. Brewster coming home?" asked Molly.

"Tomorrow," he said. "I'm taking Nathan over to the hospital now to meet Charlotte and see Mommy, and we'll come back later for a nap. I know *I* could use one! See you later!"

"Bye-bye!" said Nathan, waving.

"Bye," said the twins. Amanda closed the door and turned to Molly. "Time for a conference call," she said, dialing Shawn's number. She and Molly loved playing with all the cool features on the phone.

"Remember, girls, the phone is not a toy," joked Molly as she imitated Dad's deep voice.

"Hello? Jordan residence," answered Shawn.

"Hi, Shawn! It's us. Hold on, we're gonna get Peichi in on this call." Soon the twins had Peichi on the line, too, and they told Shawn and Peichi the news about Charlotte.

"Mr. Brewster will be home later," said Molly. "So he'll be there when we're finished cooking."

"And it'll be a surprise!" added Amanda.

The friends decided to meet at the Moores' house to

do the cooking. And all agreed to pay dues each week for the food.

"I'm bringing some cucumbers," said Shawn. "We have too many, and they'll go bad soon."

"Okay," said Amanda. "Well, then, we could make the cucumber-and-dill soup that we made in class."

When Peichi arrived, she'd brought fresh basil from her mom's herb garden, and lettuce. "Dad bought lettuce last night," she explained. "He forgot that we already had some, so he said I could take this."

"Okay," said Molly. "That's less stuff we have to buy, then."

"Don't forget that we should buy some carrots for Nathan," Amanda reminded the girls. "He likes to eat vegetables."

The girls decided to make pesto with Mrs. Cheng's basil, along with the cucumber soup, a small green salad, and the cobbler. As the girls talked, Amanda wrote down the things they would need to buy. "This dinner won't cost us much at all," she said. "Ready to go to the store, Chef Girls?"

"Ready," replied Shawn.

"Yeah, let's go!" said Peichi. She turned to Shawn. "I can't wait to make the cucumber soup! It looked so easy in class! What should we do first? I guess we should make the soup first so we can chill it..."

Molly and Amanda smiled at each other as Peichi went on and on. An amazing summer was opening up before them. Old and new friends were around them, and every day brought exciting, unpredictable happenings.

Boredom had taken a vacation.

The Amazing Cookbook

By

The CHEF Girls

AMANDA!

Molly!

Peichi ☺

shawn!

Mrs. Moore's Easy and Delicious Pesto Sauce

2 cups fresh basil leaves (make sure you rinse
    them and dry them off in the salad spinner, and cut
    off the stems)
1 clove garlic, peeled and crushed
2 tablespoons pine nuts, lightly
    toasted in a small heavy
    skillet on top of stove
1/2 cup extra-virgin olive oil
Dash of salt
1/2 cup grated Parmesan cheese

Put the basil, garlic, toasted pine nuts, salt,
and about half the oil in a blender or a food
processor. Turn it on (of course!). Add the
rest of the oil slowly. (Ask an adult to help
you use the machine, says Mrs. Moore!)
Make sure to scrape down the sides with
a spatula once in a while, to get everything
            mixed (turn off the machine for this part).
            Stir in the grated Parmesan cheese
            right before serving.
                Put the pesto on top of cooked

pasta. Serve to your family, friends, and adoring fans!

this can keep in the refrigerator for up to two weeks!

Hi, it's Peichi now! My mom makes pesto, too, with the basil from our herb garden. She freezes it. But you have to make sure that you don't freeze it if it has Parmesan cheese in it. The cheese won't taste good if you freeze it in the pesto. Okay? ☺

I LOVE SUMMER BECAUSE mom MAKES COBBLERS FOR
DESSERT! THIS IS OUR FAVORITE BECAUSE OF THE
SUGAR COOKIE CRUST. AND WE LOVE THE TASTE OF
BLUEBERRIES AND NECTARINES TOGETHER. PUT VANILLA
ICE CREAM ON TOP. EVERYONE WILL LOVE IT!!!!

—AMANDA

mom's AND AMANDA'S FAVORITE COBBLER

YOU WILL NEED:

A 13 X 9" BAKING PAN

4 NECTARINES, RINSED, CUT INTO CHUNKS

3 TO 4 CUPS BLUEBERRIES, RINSED

3/4 CUP ORANGE JUICE

1/3 CUP SUGAR

1 TABLESPOON PLUS 2 TEASPOONS CORNSTARCH

1 CUP (2 STICKS) UNSALTED BUTTER, SOFTENED

1 CUP SUGAR

1/2 TEASPOON BAKING POWDER

1/2 TEASPOON SALT

I got this recipe from my Aunt Hazel, who grew up in the South. It's a famous Southern recipe. You can use peaches instead of nectarines. You don't need to peel nectarines, but you will need to peel peaches. Happy eating!

—Mom

1 LARGE EGG

1 TEASPOON PURE VANILLA EXTRACT

1 CUP FLOUR (MEASURE THE FLOUR VERY CAREFULLY WITH A SPOON INTO THE MEASURING CUP. MOM SAYS NEVER PACK FLOUR, OKAY?)

PREHEAT THE OVEN TO 375 DEGREES.

COMBINE THE FRUIT, ORANGE JUICE, CORN STARCH AND 1/3 CUP SUGAR IN THE PAN. MIX IT GENTLY.

NOW MAKE THE SUGAR-COOKIE CRUST. ALL YOU NEED TO DO IS COMBINE THE BUTTER, 1 CUP SUGAR, BAKING POWDER, AND SALT IN A MIXING BOWL. MASH IT WITH THE BACK OF A

WOODEN SPOON UNTIL IT'S BLENDED.

NOW ADD THE EGG AND VANILLA. BEAT IT UNTIL IT'S CREAMY. THEN STIR IN THE FLOUR UNTIL IT'S COMBINED.

DROP THE BATTER IN SPOONFULS ON TOP OF THE FRUIT. DON'T SMOOTH IT ALL OVER THE FRUIT; THE GLOBS OF BATTER WILL BECOME ONE SMOOTH TOPPING IN THE OVEN. TRUST ME! ☺

BAKE FOR 40 TO 50 MINUTES, OR UNTIL THE CRUST IS GOLDEN BROWN. AFTER YOU TAKE IT OUT OF THE OVEN, LET IT COOL 10 TO 30 MINUTES. THEN CUT IT UP AND SERVE.

143

Carmen's tomato sauce with Fresh Herbs

this is easy! In class we used fresh tomatoes, but you can also use canned tomatoes like the Chef Girls did today (it saved time).

3 cloves garlic, gently smashed with a fork
3 tablespoons olive oil
1 can whole plum tomatoes (28 ounces)
salt and pepper
3 tablespoons fresh basil leaves, minced

(that means chopped into very small pieces...aah!
Love that smell!)

Heat 2 tablespoons of the olive oil and the garlic over medium-low heat in a skillet. Stir once in a while until the garlic is lightly cooked.

Drain the tomatoes. You can remove the seeds, if there are any. (Some people don't, but we did. Do what you want, it's a free country!)

Crush the tomatoes (use a fork), and add them to the skillet. Put in the basil, and a dash of salt and pepper.

Raise the heat to medium-high and stir once in a while until the tomatoes thicken. (This will probably take 10 minutes. Be patient!) Now it's turning into sauce! Cool! Stir in the rest of the oil, and add some more salt, a little at a time, if you think it's necessary. That's it! Then you pour it over the cooked pasta (duh!). You can put more fresh minced basil on top. It looks pretty!

cooking tips from the chef Girls!

The Chef Girls are looking out for you!
Here are some things you should
know if you want to cook.
(Remember to ask your parents
if can use knives and the stove!)

1   Tie back long hair so that it won't
    get into the food or in the way as
    you work.

2   Don't wear loose-fitting clothing
    that could drag in the food or
    on the stove burners.

3   Never cook in bare feet or open-toed
    shoes. Something sharp or hot could
    drop on your feet.

4   Always wash your hands before you
    handle food.

5   Read through the recipe before you start. Gather your ingredients together and measure them before you begin.

6   Turn pot handles in so that they won't get knocked off the stove.

7   Use wooden spoons to stir hot liquids. Metal spoons can become very hot.

8   When cutting or peeling food, cut away from your hands.

9   Cut food on a cutting board, not the countertop.

 10   Hand someone a knife with the knifepoint pointing to the floor.

11   Clean up as you go. It's safer and neater.

12   Always use a dry pot holder to remove something hot from the oven. You could get burned with a wet one, since wet ones retain heat.

13   Make sure that any spills on the floor are cleaned up right away, so that you don't slip and fall.

14 Don't put knives in clean-up water. You could reach into the water and cut yourself.

15 Use a wire rack to cool hot baking dishes, to avoid scorch marks on the countertop

An Important Message from the Chef Girls!

Some foods can carry bacteria, such as salmonella, that can make you sick. To avoid salmonella, always cook poultry, ground beef, and eggs thoroughly before eating. Don't eat or drink foods containing raw eggs. And wash hands, kitchen work surfaces, and utensils with soap and water immediately after they have been in contact with raw meat or poultry.

148

Wuzzup What's up?

:-@ surprise or shock

GMTA Great Minds Think Alike

LOL Laughing Out Loud

G2G Got To Go

b-b Bye-Bye

L8R Later, as in "See ya later!"

Mwa smooching sound

Here's a sneak peak at:

dish #2

Turning Up the Heat

friends, cooking, eating, talking, life.

Molly and Amanda Moore were hanging 130 feet in the air. Swaying back and forth under the hot sun. Going nowhere on a Ferris wheel that was older than their grandparents.

"*Aaaagh!*" cried Molly. The twins' caged car suddenly dipped, rolled back up, and stopped with a jolt.

"I can't look down," whispered Amanda, Molly's twin. "I feel sick. Stop this thing!"

"It *has* stopped," Molly replied. "You can open your eyes now, Manda!"

Amanda squeezed her eyes shut even tighter.

"Come on, we have a great view of the ocean from up here!" Molly said.

Amanda shook her head.

"Anyway," continued Molly, "you shouldn't have had an entire hero. Or the saltwater taffy after that!"

"I know," Amanda mumbled. "Don't remind me."

Suddenly, the car dipped.

"*Whoa!*" Amanda shouted. Her face turned almost as green as her T-shirt. She grabbed her sister's arm. Hard.

"Ouch!" yelled Molly. "Your *nails!*"

"Sorry," Amanda said, loosening her grip.

The Ferris wheel, or Wonder Wheel, as it was called at Coney Island in Brooklyn, New York, stopped again.

"Hey, look!" said Molly. "I see Shawn and Peichi." She waved to their friends down on the ground. "I think they're laughing at us!"

"Now I know why they didn't get on with us. They've been on it before," Amanda said.

Finally, the girls' car made it to the bottom.

"Get me out of here!" cried Amanda as the tattooed ride operator unlocked the car door.

"Okay. I feel better now," announced Amanda, taking a deep breath of air.

"Come on," Molly said, poking her sister. "Tell me you didn't have a *little* fun. I mean, Mom rode this same ride when she was a kid. That's kind of cool, isn't it? "

Amanda shrugged and put on her shades. She looked toward the boardwalk. "Where'd Shawn and Peichi go?" she asked. "I don't see Mr. Jordan, either." Mr. Jordan was Shawn's dad.

Molly stood up on her toes and stretched her neck. "I see them. They're talking to someone, but I can't tell who." Molly grabbed her sister's arm and pulled her through a group of rowdy kids, and up a ramp to the boardwalk. They found Peichi and Shawn talking to Connor and Omar, two boys they knew from their summer cooking class, and a bored-looking teenager who was probably Omar's brother. Mr. Jordan was a few yards away, in line to buy something to drink.

"Hi!" called Peichi as the twins got closer. "Omar was just telling us that there's a sideshow around the corner!"

"A *side*show?" Molly asked. "What's that?"

"It's like a theatre, but really wacko! It's called Sideshows by the Seashore." Omar explained.

"Yeah," Peichi said. "They saw this guy, he had tattoos all over, even on his *face*, and he hammered a nail into his tongue!"

"*Oooh*, gross," exclaimed Amanda.

"No way," said Molly, rolling her eyes. "It's a trick!"

"No it isn't!" insisted Omar. He looked at Connor for help. "Tell them, Connor!"

Connor nodded. "He really did it!" he exclaimed. "Go see him! He's called The Human Blockhead. He eats glass, too! And there's other cool stuff. Like a snake charmer who walks around wearing this humongo python."

151

Shawn shuddered. "Get outta here!" she exclaimed. "Is it alive?"

"Oh, yeah!" replied Connor. "It's the fattest, longest, biggest snake I've ever seen."

"Check it out," suggested Omar. Then he nodded at his big brother, who was beginning to look impatient, and said to the girls, "We gotta go. Later."

"See you in class," said Molly and Amanda. They looked at each other and laughed. They were doing their "twin thing" again. That's what they called saying the same thing at the same time, or reading each other's minds.

"Yeah, later," said Connor. "Let's get something to eat, guys." The boys walked off.

Shawn turned to the girls and giggled. "I hope they don't go home and try eating glass!"

"Let's check out the sideshow!" cried Peichi. She looked around at all the girls. "Do you think your dad would take us, Shawn?"

Shawn giggled. "I doubt it. It doesn't sound like the kind of thing my dad would want me to see! He'd probably make that *face*." She raised one eyebrow and pursed her lips, imitating how Mr. Jordan looked when he didn't approve of something.

Molly dug into the pockets of her cutoffs. "We're out of money, anyway," she announced, looking at Amanda. "We can't do anything else unless it's free!"

"We can walk on the beach," suggested Mr. Jordan, who came up behind the girls and handed out cold bottles of water. "That's free. Come on, I'll take a picture of you."

"Great!" exclaimed Peichi. "I'm so *hot!* I can't wait to put my feet into the water!" She reached down to take off her sandals.

Holding their shoes, the girls followed Mr. Jordan down the steps from the boardwalk. Their feet sank into the sand.

"*Ouch!* The sand's burning my feet!" cried Shawn. She began to run toward the water, and everyone followed her, dodging sunbathers lying on their towels. Finally, the friends reached the ocean, and they turned around to face Mr. Jordan. They put their arms around each other, shrieking at the feel of the cold water rushing over their feet.

Click! went the camera.

"Work it, girls!" joked Mr. Jordan. He kneeled on the sand and pretended to be a fashion photographer as the friends posed and laughed. *Click! Click!*

I hope Shawn gives us copies of these pictures, thought Molly, *to remember this summer by.*

"We're gonna get something to eat at Nathan's restaurant," called Shawn. "Come on! Dad's treating everyone!"

The girls ran along the sand back to the boardwalk, and put on their shoes for the quick walk to Surf Avenue. It was time for one of the best things about Coney Island—the hot dogs!

"I love hot dogs," stated Mr. Jordan, once everyone had filed into Nathan's Famous. "Did you know that the hot dog was invented over 130 years ago? And Nathan's has been here since 1916! That's when they held the first July 4th hot-dog eating contest." He pointed at some old photos on the wall. "See, here's Nathan's way back when...look at all the men wearing suits, and the ladies in their big hats and long dresses and shawls. Can you believe that's what people wore to the beach back then?"

"Weren't they *hot?*" asked Peichi.

Molly giggled. "Mr. Jordan, you know *everything.*"

"Well, I just think all this stuff is interesting," said Mr. Jordan. He turned to Shawn and smiled. "I'm not embarrassing you, am I Shawn?"

Shawn smiled shyly and looked down. He could read her mind! "No, Dad."

Mr. Jordan was always embarrassing Shawn somehow. But Shawn loved her dad more than anything. She was proud of him, too. He had written a book. It was a history book about jazz music in New Orleans. Shawn liked reading sections of it from time to time, and looking at the photo of her dad on the book jacket. Like Molly's and Amanda's mom, Mr. Jordan was a college professor. And he could also play the guitar, a cool type of music called the blues.

"Here's our order," said Mr. Jordan. "Quick, let's grab those two tables."

Everyone brought their food to the tables in front of a window. Actually, the tables were more like tall, round counters.

"How come there aren't any seats?" Amanda wanted to know.

Mr. Jordan laughed. "This is fast food—they want you in and out, so the next customer can come in!"

"*Mmmm,* this is great," said Peichi. She licked off some bright yellow mustard from the corner of her mouth. "I've never had a Nathan's hot dog before!"

"*Never?*" asked Mr. Jordan. He dropped his mouth open, pretending to be shocked. "A Brooklyn girl like yourself? Well, young lady, it's about time you did! How about another?"

"Um—okay! That would be great!" replied Peichi. Everyone laughed. No one could ever accuse *her* of being shy.

"Anybody else want anything?" asked Mr. Jordan, looking at each girl. "Shawn? No? What about you, Amanda? You're always game for seconds!"

"That's for sure," Molly said, rolling her eyes.

"I'd better not, Mr. Jordan," replied Amanda. "I've had a lot of stuff here today. But thank you."

"Molly?" asked Mr. Jordan. "How about you?"

Molly smiled. "No thanks, Mr. Jordan," she replied. "I'm stuffed."

"Suit yourself," said Mr. Jordan. "Peichi, I guess it's just you and me!"

As Mr. Jordan walked to the counter, Shawn's dark brown eyes followed him.

"He seems to be, um, more like—himself now," said Molly awkwardly. "The way he used to be."

"What?" asked Shawn, turning back to look at Molly.

Amanda spoke up. "Your dad seems, you know, happier now."

Shawn smiled, a little sadly. "Yeah. I think he's feeling a little better these days." The friends saw tears well up in Shawn's eyes, behind her purple cat glasses. "But you know, he still misses my mom," she quickly added.

"Of course," said Molly. She, Amanda, and Peichi nodded understandingly. "He always will, Shawn. But it's good that he's doing better now."

No one said anything.

Molly cleared her throat. "So, Mom's birthday is the day after tomorrow," she said, changing the subject. "What are we doing for her?"

Amanda shrugged. "I don't know," she said. "Dad hasn't said much about it. She'll probably just want to go out to dinner."

Molly's face lit up. "We should have a surprise party for her!" she said.

"Yeah! You should!" said Peichi. "That's a great idea!"

A surprise party? Amanda was thinking. *But surprise parties are so hard to keep secret. Plus, they're really hard to plan.*

"You could have it in the garden," suggested Shawn. "And you could have—"

"Hot dogs!" interrupted Molly with a giggle. "It could be a cookout."

The three girls looked at Amanda as if to say, *Well? What do you think?*

"Yeah, a cookout," she said slowly. "That's what I was going to say." She didn't want to be the only one who thought it would be too hard to do. Mr. Jordan, who'd returned with the hot dogs, gave her a quick smile. He seemed to understand how she felt.

"You could come to Mom's party, too, Mr. Jordan," said Amanda. Mr. Jordan and Mom had known each other since high school.

"Thank you!" he said. "But I think you two need to check with your dad first and see what he's planning."

Molly giggled. "You know what? He probably forgot about Mom's birthday. Dad's kind of like that."

Amanda smiled. "Yeah, it's true," she said.

"My dad's like that, too!" said Peichi. "My mom has to write everything down for him on a big calendar we keep in the kitchen."

"Well," said Molly, "I think this calls for an emergency meeting of the fabulous Chef Girls! Manda and I can't do this party without you."

That's for sure, thought Amanda.

"Dad will pay for Mom's party," said Molly. "So we can meet tomorrow for sure. Hey, I know! We *can* have the party tomorrow. That way Mom will be *really* surprised!"

Tomorrow! Uh-oh! thought Amanda. *Why am I the only one who thinks this is a big deal? I don't think I want to do this!*

After Nathan's, it was time to cross Surf Avenue and get on the subway. This part of the subway line was elevated, instead of being underground. The girls liked seeing Brooklyn from above for a change. At the foot of the subway stairs, they passed Philip's Candy Store.

"Last chance for frozen chocolate-covered bananas!" called Mr. Jordan, waving at the man behind the counter. "This candy store has been here for over forty years! I used to come here when I was a kid and get the taffy apples." He paused on the stairs. "I can't think of anywhere else in the world where you can take the subway to the ocean," he remarked. "Except Tokyo, Japan. I know you can do that in Japan."

"That's my dad, the walking encyclopedia," Shawn said and she slid her MetroCard through the slot on the turnstile. "Oh! I hear the train!"

"Hurry up!" said Molly.

Everyone hurried up the ramp toward the train. They could hear a conductor announce, "Stand clear of the closing doors." The doors would close soon.

"Let's not rush, girls, there's always another train," said Mr. Jordan, but Molly and Amanda were sprinting toward the doors. "Hurry, Amanda!" Molly was saying to Amanda, who was slightly ahead.

"Slow down, girls!" shouted Mr. Jordan, running to keep up.

Shawn and Peichi were sprinting now, too, behind Mr. Jordan. Just then, the doors closed. Molly, Mr. Jordan, Shawn, and Peichi didn't make it on the train.

Amanda pressed against the doors, but they didn't open.

She couldn't believe it! Molly had made her rush. And she didn't even give her a warning that she wasn't getting on. Her mind was probably on that dumb surprise party!

Amanda saw Mr. Jordan mouth. "Get off at the next stop."

Amanda nodded as her train rolled out of the station, away from all of her friends.